I0775431

Just One Take

THE BILLIONAIRE BARONS OF TEXAS · BOOK FOUR

CHRIS KENISTON

Indie House Publishing

Indie House Publishing

MORE BOOKS
By Chris Keniston

The Billionaire Barons of Texas
Just One Date
Just One Spark
Just One Dance
Just One Take
Just One Taste
Just One Shot
Just One Chance

Hart Land
Heather
Lily
Violet
Iris
Hyacinth
Rose
Calytrix
Zinnia
Poppy
Picture Perfect

Farraday Country
Adam
Brooks
Connor
Declan
Ethan
Finn
Grace
Hannah
Ian
Jamison

Keeping Eileen
Loving Chloe
Morgan
Neil
Owen

Honeymoon Series

Honeymoon for One
Honeymoon for Three
Honeymoon for Four
Honeymoon for Five

Aloha Romance Series:

Aloha Texas
Almost Paradise
Mai Tai Marriage
Dive Into You
Look of Love
Love by Design
Love Walks In
Shell Game
Flirting with Paradise

Surf's Up Flirts:
(Aloha Series Companions)

Shall We Dance
Love on Tap
Head Over Heels
Perfect Match
Just One Kiss
It Had to Be You
Cat's Meow

CHAPTER ONE

No one ever mentioned how young old age starts. Craig Baron took a long swallow of cool water. Rebuilding the bull-proof fence line between the Baron and Gold ranches was proving to be a bit more challenging than any of the brothers had expected.

"The old gray mare, she ain't what she used to be," Chase sang to his younger brother, a huge grin on his face. "Growing older isn't for sissies."

"Pot calling the kettle black?" Leaning on the shovel handle, Craig straightened his shoulders. "And for the record, I am neither old, nor a sissy." He wasn't even going to address the mis-assigned gender of mare.

"Speak for yourself." The eldest of today's workers, his brother Mitch pulled a traditional bandana from his back pocket and wiped his brow. "I freely admit this was way easier a decade ago."

"Ditto." Kyle, the sibling most likely to be in the best physical condition, chugged a bottle of water, then squeezing it, he tossed it into the nearby bin. "I think fence digging is for the next generation."

"And car racing?" One brow arched high on Jared Gold's—soon to be an official member of the Baron clan thanks to Craig's sister Eve—forehead.

Kyle blew out a long sigh. "It's not official yet, but," his gaze lifted to a point in the distance, "I think it's time to hang up my helmet."

Having taken another long gulp of water, Craig almost spit out his drink. His entire life, every single Baron family member had a competitive streak as wide as the Nile. Each and every one of them strived to be at the top of their game, no matter what it took to get there. The idea of Kyle walking away from racing was as absurd as Craig walking away from an award-winning film. Not happening. "Are you kidding?"

"Nope." Kyle removed his hat and slapped the dust off against his thigh before placing it back on his head. "I think it's time."

"Wow." Mitch shook his head. "I know you've been hinting at it, but didn't expect to see it actually happen. At least not yet."

"Like I said," Kyle grabbed hold of one side of the two man auger for digging deeper postholes, "nothing's official yet. Might need to give Gibs another year."

"Unless someone moves over." Craig waved his fingers. "I've heard rumors that Bergeron isn't happy with his team. He's not as good as you, but he's close."

"Hmm," Kyle muttered.

From what Craig could see, his brother might think he was ready to hang up his racing suit, but maybe not so much ready to be replaced. Heaven knew Craig and Kyle weren't that far apart in years, and yet Craig was just beginning to reap the benefits of his hard work. Making it to the top of the movie industry was not any easier than climbing to the top of the racing world. He couldn't fathom Kyle walking away any more than he could fathom not fighting tooth and nail for that next big film that would make Baron Productions the holy grail of the industry. The company that A-listers would be chasing after him to produce instead of the other way around. Biting his tongue, he shook his head. No way could Kyle walk away.

Jared took a minute to survey their work for the day, then glanced up at the sky. "Heat's starting to bear down on us."

"This is Texas," sarcasm dripped from Kyle's words. "The heat is always bearing down on us."

Jared chuckled. "True, but in today's case, I think we've made nice progress. This would be a good place to call it a day and pick up again tomorrow."

Craig's back twinged at the mere mention of doing this

again tomorrow. He really had let his desk job make him soft. "I admit, right about now, Hazel's French cream crumb cake and a cool glass of blueberry lemonade sounds heavenly."

Staring off into the distance, Mitch's head whipped around. "Hazel made French cream crumb cake?"

The man had his moments. Just when Craig thought his older brother was totally in his own little world, he'd perk up and let everyone know he was right in step with the conversation even if he'd not said a word. The man had also been spending a great deal more of his time at the ranch than usual. Mitch would fly back and forth to DC to conduct Senate business, and then scurry home again for as long as he could. Every last member of the family considered the ranch home base and on any given weekend at least half of them would arrive and settle into their old rooms as if not a day had passed since their childhoods spending summers and weekends with the grandparents. Still, Craig wasn't sure when was the last time Mitch had made even a short pit stop at his downtown home. Almost every weekend, sometimes weekdays too, he could be found in the barns.

Despite their best efforts to subtly uncover what, if anything, was bothering Mitch, none of the brothers had been able to learn why he was spending more time than usual on the ranch the last few months. The ache beginning to poke at Craig's lower back reminded him that about now a good hot shower was in order. He could pick up worrying about his big brother another day.

"Last one back to the ranch is a rotten egg." Of course Kyle had to reduce everything to a race. The man might think he was ready to retire from the adrenaline rush of the racing world, but Craig was yet to be convinced.

In record time the entire family made it back to the ranch for that long hot shower, a change into clean clothes, and a short respite before dinner with the Governor and Grams. Even Jared and Eve joined them for the family meal.

"Any news on a date yet?" stroking the pup nestled at

her side, their grandmother casually asked her granddaughter. Much the same way she'd managed to ask every week since Jared got down in front of the entire family on bended knee and proposed.

"I want to look at a few more halls before we narrow down availabilities," Eve answered just as casually as she had each and every other time her grandmother had asked the same question.

The truth was that he knew his sister was still waiting on their mother to give Eve a window when she could abandon her hideaway in Europe to brave another family wedding. Since tension tended to run high when it came to the Barons and their mother—the first ex Mrs. Bradley Baron—his sweet kid sister willingly took the flack.

"I understand Paige's plans for making the winery available as a wedding venue are coming along well. Perhaps that would be a good fit?" His grandmother's dimples deepened as the corners of her mouth lifted into a teasing smile. "I could pull a few strings if you like."

Eve's broad grin widened to match her grandmother's. "I might have a few strings of my own I could pull."

"What strings are we pulling now?" Paige, the aforementioned sister—daughter of the second ex Mrs. Bradley Baron—fluttered into the room, immediately planting a kiss on her grandmother's cheek.

Smiling up at her granddaughter, Lila Baron waved her arm at Eve. "For a wedding at the vineyard."

Paige's gaze whipped around to Eve. "You interested?"

Lips pressed tightly together, the corners of Eve's mouth began to tip upward as she bobbed her head slowly. "Maybe."

Slapping her hands together with enthusiasm, Paige took her seat and leveling her gaze with her older sister, waved a finger at her. "After dinner. We'll talk."

The two siblings grinned at each other like the little girls at the table he remembered from so long ago. Though he knew there had been a lot of discussion on Paige's ambitions for the family winery, somehow, he hadn't realized she'd made enough progress to host a Baron family wedding.

"Where are you filming this week?" The Governor sliced his beef tenderloin, and stabbing at the piece, held it on the fork dangling in midair, waiting for Craig's response.

"Vancouver."

"Long flight."

Craig nodded. Didn't he know it. As Executive Producer he didn't need to be on set for filming every minute of every day, but his grandfather had taught him a long time ago that the only way to get ahead of the next guy was to work twice as hard. Besides that, the old man had also taught them all that the best way to avoid unpleasant surprises was to always keep at least one eye on any project. Whether business or pleasure, Craig had done just that, and more than once it had saved his bacon.

"Any luck with that option you were telling us about?"

Craig had to think which the heck option was his grandfather talking about.

"You know," his grandfather continued, as if he'd read Craig's mind, "that actress who lives near Austin that you were so excited about."

Oh yes. The difficult diva who had moved to Hill Country over a decade ago after completing one of her many blockbuster movies. The woman no longer considered starring in movies filmed outside of her state, *and* just happened to own the rights to the hottest commodity out there at the moment. The potential golden goose. A slam dunk for an Oscar nomination if handled correctly, which his production company would do, and the movie that would be the ultimate deal to put him at the top. "Still a negotiation in progress."

"Texas studio still the sticking point?" Holding a glass of water, the Governor lifted it to his lips in a show of casual chit-chat when in fact, much like his grandmother's approach to Eve's wedding, there was nothing casual at all about the question.

Craig nodded. One of many where this particular diva was concerned.

"A studio closer to home wouldn't be a bad thing. Give it any more thought?"

"Some." That was most likely not the response his grandfather wanted, but it was the truth. Or at least part of the truth. With productions often running simultaneously all across the country, and his constantly catching red-eye flights to keep up, he'd more than thought about it. Including the expense and headache of undertaking the kind of project he would need, especially his preferred location in or near Houston and the ranch—a part of the country that was virtually a production desert. Austin was closer to his condo, but considering he spent more free time at the ranch than his own place, and that the cost and availability of land in the popular metroplex was beyond prohibitive, even for a Baron, that option was out of the question. Which left the idea of instead focusing on Dallas, a city that would bring him closer to his brother Chase, and that already had a healthy pool of industry professionals. Despite the head start the North Texas location offered, he couldn't bring himself to be enthused about driving four hours to visit family and the ranch any more than sitting on a plane for that amount of time. So instead, he'd done his best to charm the diva out of Texas—so far to no avail.

"You do know that the legislature has just passed approval for new tax incentives for just this type of project?"

He couldn't help but lift his gaze to meet his grandfather's. Honestly, he hadn't paid any attention to whether or not the State of Texas had perks lined up for such a project. "I'll have to look into it."

The Governor gave a single dip of his chin. "There's a folder with the highlights in my office. If you're interested, you can take a look after dinner. There also may be a few property suggestions your cousin Devlin left in the same folder."

Again, Craig nodded. Whether he was interested or not, which he was most definitely at least curious, a suggestion from the Governor might as well have been a military order. The civilian equivalent of *voluntold*. The military concept of being told to volunteer was not lost on his family. Of course, now the question that ricocheted in his mind was whether or not this particular idea would be the Holy Grail solution to his travel exhaustion and negotiation frustrations, or a suicide mission.

"Next time anyone shouts road trip after a plethora of chocolate martinis, remind me to insist we at least stay in the state of Texas." Kathleen Elizabeth Donovan, more commonly known by Kate, was most definitely a through and through extrovert with a side of gypsy. She was also getting too old to sit in a car for most of the day after joining her friends on a spontaneous trip across two states.

"Are you saying you didn't like the hot springs?" Joan, her best friend since kindergarten, didn't bother to take her attention away from the road ahead. Most likely because Joan already knew the answer.

"You know I loved every relaxing minute." And she had. Whether it was the refrigerator that insisted on freezing your milk, the neighbor's teen whose high school band chose the middle of your online meeting to practice Metallica songs, badly, or some moron who didn't understand why you couldn't play with nesting sea turtles, some days life just came at you from every direction. Not till three whole days in the peace and quiet that Mother Nature intended and all the little critters that came with it did Kate realize just how draining the real world had become. "We really do need to escape more often."

"Amen to that. Though it would help if you spent at least a fraction of the time you spend saving the world on pampering yourself."

"Maybe." She couldn't say much more, after all, Joan had a good point. For as long as Kate could remember, she worried more about helpless and abandoned animals than humans. Not everyone had the privilege of growing up and making their passion their career. She just wished having become a successful environmentalist didn't include having to deal with the money loving, profit above all, side of society. Preserving at risk species and their natural environment had proven to be a lot more demanding than fostering a few abandoned kittens when she was nine. Even so, she wouldn't change a thing—except maybe from now on a few more girls' weekends away.

Less than an hour from home, the computerized voice of the GPS stiffly instructed them to take the next exit. A quick glance at the map and the long line of orange then red along the freeway explained why. Within moments of the redirection, traffic began to slow just as they approached the suggested exit.

Joan shook her head and sighed. "I suppose the extra twenty minutes this little detour is going to cost us is less than the time we'd lose if we stayed on the freeway."

"No doubt." For the next few minutes, they followed the service road and could see the parking lot the freeway had become. "I feel sorry for those folks. From the looks of it, they're going to be sitting there a good long while."

"Thank heavens for whoever invented GPS. I think I'll have a glass of wine when we get home in his—or her—honor."

"Ditto." Kate chuckled. Her head resting back against the seat, she took in the spray of pinks and reds and oranges splattered across the sky as the sun lowered itself behind the treetop canopy ahead. The little detour had taken them far from the freeway and deep into the countryside. It had been ages since she'd seen so many stars in the evening sky. Light pollution in Houston had hidden the stars for as long as she could remember.

Keeping her gaze on the treetops under the moonlight, a bird in flight caught her eye. The wingspread was impressive and the graceful movement of the bird soaring about brought a smile to her face. For Kate, watching nature's animals roam, or in this case fly, free in their natural habitat was as relaxing as the time they'd spent soaking in the natural hot springs. Her heart beat happily when what she now realized was an owl, landed on a low-hanging branch down the road.

"Did you see that?" Joan waved an arm in the direction of the owl.

"I did. Magnificent."

As they grew closer, Joan's car was nearly underneath him when Kate realized which species of owl had been putting on a show for them. If she wasn't mistaken, this particular owl was one of the endangered breeds on a protective list in Texas. Mostly because to the best of her knowledge, these guys rarely ventured west of Louisiana. As if the birds had a visible map to follow, they almost always stopped at the state line.

"Ooh, there he goes." Arm extended, Joan's finger dangled in the direction the bird had flown.

Taking in a deep sigh, Kate knew she needed to follow up on the bird. Every instinct she had, and she had good ones when it came to wildlife, she knew she needed to determine where this bird was calling home. Her arm straight and her finger extended, she pointed at a dirt road just beyond the tree. "Follow that bird."

Joan slowed and for the first time since turning off the freeway onto the lonely, dark, unlit country road, turned to Kate. "You've got to be kidding?"

Shaking her head vehemently, she continued to point ahead. "I have to find out of he's tagged and protected."

Joan's deep sigh filled the small car. "I guess I should be thankful you didn't find any endangered animals before we crossed the state line. I mean, I'm assuming the reason we're following that poor bird is because it's endangered?"

"Maybe."

This time deep creases filled Joan's forehead as she turned off the two-lane road. "Please don't tell me you feel like bird-watching for the heck of it?"

"Of course not."

"You do know that you're off duty, right?"

"No such thing." Saving the planet was not a nine to five job like a receptionist at a law firm. She cared about all the animals everywhere, even if she couldn't help them all.

"Right." Joan winced as her budget sedan bounced over the unleveled dirt. "Oh, I hope we don't need AAA. They'll never find us out here."

For a moment, Kate lost sight of the owl and then, as if

he knew she was looking for him, the bird did a near dive and flew across the front of their car.

"I'm guessing this is private property." Joan practically hugged the steering wheel as she scanned their surroundings and winced louder with each pothole they hit. "If some old geezer comes out and shoots me, you get to explain to my parents why this bird is so important."

For a brief moment the visual of an aging rancher with a corn-cob pipe, overalls, and a shotgun the size of Texas almost had Kate reconsidering the folly of their pursuit. Almost. "I'm sure we'll be fine. Any self-respecting rancher or farmer went to bed with the chickens."

"I sure hope they know that."

"There!" Kate pointed to cluster of buildings across an overgrown field that the owl had disappeared into. "That must be where she's nesting."

"I thought it was a he?" Joan's voice squealed as her car did another bounce.

"He, she, does it matter?"

"Only to its mate." The tease was back in her friend's banter.

Now all she had to figure out was how in the heck were they going to cross the field and find his or her nest in the pitch of night? And more importantly, without Joan killing her!

CHAPTER TWO

Folder open in his lap, Craig shook his head. "Notes? The Governor is certainly the master of understatement."

Having joined them late last night, his cousin Devlin chuckled from behind the wheel of the ranch jeep. "I gather our beloved grandfather didn't mention that he's had me working on this for over a week."

"All he said was you had some notes." The stack of properties that Devlin had mapped out for them to visit was more like an encyclopedia. Reading the information on the listings, it had been easy for Craig to discard at least a handful. So far they'd walked two vacant warehouses in an older section south of downtown and too close to hurricane country for his liking. Not that hurricane season hadn't been a fact of life during his childhood. One that most folks ignored much the way North Texas failed to harp on tornado alley or California on the San Andreas Fault. Weather happened. Still, he didn't want to test Mother Nature's temper.

"Exactly how far outside of the loop do you want to venture?" Dev glanced at his GPS. The next property was in an underdeveloped part of old Klein. What must have once been the center of the small community had fallen into disrepair. The one building that was potentially large enough for the basic studio facilities he'd need to move some productions to his home state was appealing, but so were some of the other vacant locations. Even though he couldn't buy a property or start a venture over one potential film deal for one Texas star, if he wanted to win her over, none of the city warehouse locations would be diverse enough for the kind of film he knew the diva wanted.

"You have that look in your eye." His cousin didn't even glance in his direction.

"And what look would that be?"

Dev barely turned long enough to roll his eyes at Craig. "The one that says any minute I can expect a crazy idea."

"Why does it have to be crazy?"

Shaking his head, his cousin smiled. "Remember who you're talking to. I've been on one side or the other of many of your bright ideas and that particular glint in your eyes only happens with your more elaborate schemes."

"But profitable?" For the most part the more outside the box the idea, the more risk, and the more risk, the more profit. So far his record was nearly perfect.

Dev shrugged. "Expanding that one time dilapidated roadside hotel into the golf club resort was definitely a home run for Baron Enterprises."

"And it was me who gave Chase the idea to centralize the home office."

"True, though the high-rise tower was his idea."

"And a good one."

"But the mining venture, not so much."

The family coffers had taken a slight hit with that project. In the end they'd had to let it go at a slight loss.

"So." Dev shifted in the driver's seat of his SUV. "Do I want to know what you're thinking?"

"I'm wondering if it wouldn't make more sense to move a bit further out of town, close enough for crew and other personnel to commute, but far enough out that we could build a studio that would draw other film-makers as well. You know, like that town where they filmed *The Alamo*."

Keeping his gaze on the road, Dev frowned. "Explain."

"Is there an old town for sale anywhere?"

Dev's brows shot up high on his forehead. "Town?"

"Nothing too big. Something that could be used for filming street scenes for low-budget movies or TV shows."

"A town?" Dev repeated.

Craig nodded.

It took another long minute of silence before his cousin

turned to him and smiled. "You almost had me on that one. Good joke."

"I'm not joking."

Dev sucked in a deep breath. "No, I don't know of any towns for sale."

"Can you find one?"

The furrows between his cousin's brows grew deeper and one hand lifted away from the steering wheel to rub them away. "I honestly don't know."

"Okay. What about some old ranch? You know, not as big as Paradise Ridge but with plenty of buildings. Maybe in disrepair but would need more than a strong wind to knock it over?"

His cousin's frown seemed to suck in his whole face. His eyes narrowed, his cheeks lifted, and his lips pursed. Except for the life of him, Craig couldn't decide if there was an idea percolating or if the man was going to self combust.

Without warning, Dev pulled to the side of the road. "Give me a minute." His expression clear, he tapped at his phone, swiped at it a few more times, and then nodding, looked to Craig. "Not sure about that strong wind, but do you remember Old Man Martin?"

"The one that used to tell all those stories when we were kids about wildcatting with Gram's dad?"

"That would be the man. I got a call the other day from one of his grandsons. Seems the family spread far and wide and not till their dad passed recently did they even know they still owned a ranch in this part of the state. Even if it weren't in pretty bad shape, no one wants it."

"No one?"

"No one."

Those words for Craig were synonymous with bargain basement prices. He leaned back in his seat and grinning at his cousin, announced, "Let's make a deal."

They were on the road for a little more than half an hour when Dev turned up a dirt road that probably hadn't seen even ground in centuries. "I'm pretty sure the last vehicle to work its way down these ruts had to be a covered wagon."

Dev nodded, almost hitting his head as they went over

an unexpectedly deep pothole. "I'm inclined to agree with you."

Curiosity had taken hold. He had no idea where the boundaries began and ended, but he could safely assume all the land from the broken fence posts along the road to the crop of buildings in the distance was part of the deal. That feeling that came over him when something was very right was tickling at his cheek bones. He wasn't ready to grin yet, but he could already see the possibilities. From the traditional oversized red barn; to what had no doubt once upon a time been a smoke house; to the silo, or what was left of it; to the carriage house; to the old ranch. His mind already had designated the carriage houses as his offices. What he assumed was the main home had the mid-century look to it that folks inside the loop would have paid big bucks for regardless of condition.

"Where do you want to look first?"

The sun was already winking over the horizon. They had a window of twenty, thirty minutes tops to scan the property. The main area needed for soundstages would have to be the massive wooden structure ahead. He could even paint it Barn Red so it wouldn't be a country eyesore. "The barn."

Dev pulled up at the only section of the lot that wasn't overgrown with grass. Leaning over, he opened the glove compartment and handed his cousin a nine millimeter hand gun. "Get out here, and take this. With all this tall grass there might be a few rattlers. I'm going to turn the car around now and park in front so it will be easier getting out of Dodge."

Shaking his head, Craig gently nudged his cousin's hand, and gun, back at him. "And what if there's a family of rattlers between the front of the house and here? We both go park and we both walk to the barn."

"Has anyone ever told you you're one stubborn colt?"

"Never." He grinned, and his cousin rolled his eyes. Nothing more was said, probably because Dev knew as well as he did that he was right. No one in these parts walked tall grass without a weapon. No one.

Parked, the two exited the vehicle and searching the immediate area, Craig grabbed a nearby fallen branch, stripped a few wayward twigs, and holding it in front of him, swatted at the grass in hopes of shooing away any unwanted houseguests.

They'd barely reached the faded building leaning to one side when Dev's phone buzzed in his pocket. A quick glance and he stopped in his tracks and held up a finger. "I need to take this. You go on inside."

The last vestiges of daylight were almost completely gone. Hesitating a few moments for his eyes to adjust, he took a careful step through the open doorway. Still on its hinges, to his right, one door was firmly shut, but the barn door that should have hung at the open doorway rested against the side at an odd angle. None of which had lessened his growing interest in the property. The real test would be how far from town was this location if they were taking the more direct route.

Looking up at the rafters, he stumbled over something on the ground. A rather large something that had tangled in his feet, sending him wavering about like a massive flag dancing in the wind. Another second and he managed to upright himself and take a closer look at the offensive item that had sent him stumbling awkwardly. A sleeping bag?

And not an age-sheered remnant of long ago, but a shiny, warm, and fairly new insulated number intended for some serious camping. Glancing around the immediate area, there was a small cooler and a battery-operated lantern. What the heck? Lifting his gaze from the ground to what little he could see around him, he wished he'd thought to take the gun from Devlin. Whoever was squatting here could be as harmless as a butterfly or as dangerous as a hibernating bear woken too soon. *Crud.*

Unsure if he wanted to find out who was camping out, or just get the heck out of here and reconnoiter in full daylight, he blinked as the sun took a final dip below the horizon sending him into near pitch black. Just what he needed. Taking a step in retreat, he hoped his eyes would once again adjust to the darkness. A full moon would help, but he was pretty sure it wouldn't be tonight. Another step and he wondered why the heck, today of all days, he'd left his phone charging in Dev's car instead of putting it in his breast pocket the way he usually did. Another step and he turned on his heel, hoping to see his cousin and his phone in the distance, only to trip again.

This time he crashed into something nearly as big as him and a heck of a lot softer. Before he could mutter a gasp or word of warning, a deep loud growl echoed through the high ceilings at the same time a forceful hard surface landed at the small of his back, doubling him over in pain seconds before another object akin to the strength of a brick came down hard on the back of his neck, sending him sprawling across the ground. Right about now, a sleeping bear didn't seem so awful.

"What the heck?" a man's voice muttered over the flash of bright light that almost blinded Kate before illuminating a small swath of area in front of her. Now she could see a well-dressed man prone on the ground, but not where the voice came from. When she'd decided to come back and camp out at the barn after she and Joan had lost track of the owl, she'd been prepared to be here a good long while waiting for Mr. or Mrs. Owl to make an appearance. She had not, however, expected company to come snooping.

"Craig, are you okay?" That same voice grew louder as a shadow breached the doorway.

"Turn that thing off." Pushing to his knees, the guy on the ground kept one hand at his head and waved the other in the direction of the flashlight. "I've got a nasty little man with a hammer banging at the inside of my head and that light isn't helping any."

"Don't come any closer." She was as good a shot with a handgun as her instructor, sometimes better, but this was the first time she had to point the weapon at anything breathing. Hopefully, they couldn't see how much her hands shook, or that she still had the safety on.

Coming to his feet, one hand still hanging around his neck, his other hand up either in a gesture of surrender or blocking the light, the man muttered, "I wouldn't think of it."

"What the hell is going on?" The light from the other man's phone swung away and landed on her.

"Funny." Not really, she thought. "That's what I was wondering. Who are you and what are you doing here?"

Extending his free hand, the man with the hammering in his head reached forward. "I'm Craig Baron. This is my cousin Devlin. If you'd please put that gun away, we can explain."

Craig Baron? It had been a few hundred years since her college days. She'd forgotten many things, but the good-looking men coming and going from the townhouse down the block had not been one of them. Especially not the one from her Spanish Literature class. Squinting, she tipped her head toward the guy with the flashlight. "Shine it on his face."

The one Craig introduced as Devlin did as he was told.

"Hey," Craig nearly growled at his cousin.

She could see now it was most definitely the Craig Baron she'd met—sort of—all those years ago. Yes, he was definitely a few years older, a smidge less lanky, but there was no forgetting that face worthy of a magazine cover.

"Whose side are you on?" the prone former classmate snapped.

"The lady with the loaded gun pointed at us." The grin on Devlin's face showed no shame. As a matter of fact, she might even say it looked like Craig's cousin was enjoying the moment.

Who knew some day she'd karate chop a Baron, Craig Baron no less, in the middle of a country barn? Blowing out a deep sigh, she lowered the weapon. "Sorry about that. I'm Kate Donovan."

Craig nodded. "Apology accepted."

"Are you related to old man Martin?" Devlin asked.

Old man Martin? "Who?"

"I take it that's a no?" Craig answered for his cousin.

"Old Man Martin used to own this place. It now belongs to his heirs." Now that the coast was clear, Devlin took a step closer to his cousin, but continued speaking to her. "If you're not an heir, what are you doing here?"

"Need to take photos for the Fish and Game guy."

Craig chuckled. "I hate to point out the obvious, but there isn't water, or fish, anywhere near this place."

"I know that." She almost rolled her eyes at him. Had he been this obtuse back in college? All she'd ever seen were those smiling blue eyes that made her knees go weak no matter how far away he stood, and wavy light chestnut hair that had her itching to run her fingers through it. She was almost sorry he now wore it in a neatly cropped cut more suitable for a businessman than a college student.

"Sorry. No offense intended." Craig waved both hands at her. "But why are you working with Fish and Game?"

"The owl."

"Owl?" the two men echoed.

"Up there." Her arm pointed to the far corner where some large bird had built a nest and the owl had staked a claim to it.

The two men lifted their gaze in the direction she pointed.

"I don't see anything." Craig squinted at the dark.

"Look closer."

At that moment, the only thing visible were two bright yellow orbs that just as quickly disappeared as the bird closed his eyes again.

"He's probably unhappy with the racket y'all are making."

"Us?" Craig's eyes widened almost as round as the owl's. "We're not the ones who went all Ninja on you."

"Yeah," she winced, "I really am sorry about that."

"Well, now that we've settled that." Devlin took a step forward. "Do the Martins know you're having a slumber party with their owl?"

"It's not their owl."

"Noted. *An* owl?"

She had little choice but to shrug. Truth was she hadn't made much effort to hunt down the owners. Considering the dilapidated condition, she thought the property abandoned. "These owls and their nests are protected by federal laws."

"Well, this one can be protected somewhere else." Craig lifted his gaze to the corner where the owl had settled in.

Hands on her hips, she shook her head. "It doesn't work that way. Natural habitats cannot be disturbed."

"Maybe not, but if things go as I expect, this place will be mine in less than ten days, lock, stock and habitat, and the owl isn't welcome."

She really did not remember this guy being quite so… bossy. Yes, she knew his family had plenty of money, but apparently it came with plenty of attitude as well. Of course, sitting across the classroom from a twenty-year-old didn't exactly make for a window into his soul. "If there are eggs in that nest, you won't have a choice."

Craig's gaze narrowed slightly and for a few seconds she wondered if perhaps he had recognized her, but then his expression went completely blank and she tossed her thought aside. He brushed his hands and shook his head. "There's always a choice."

Yep, definitely did not remember him as bossy or arrogant but apparently he was both, and if he did indeed take ownership of the old barn any time soon, he was also in for a very big surprise.

CHAPTER THREE

Of all the things Craig had expected to stumble onto today, the beautiful redhead from his college Spanish Lit class was not one of them. It had definitely taken a few minutes to connect the dots. Hair cropped just above her shoulders threw him off, but even with once sparkling eyes chilled with concern, there was no mistaking that face. When realization dawned, he had no doubt this was the same redhead. He could still remember the first day of classes. After a summer of late nights and later mornings, he'd reluctantly dragged himself out of bed. Not quite ready to take on the world, he'd snapped to attention like a pedigree dog on point as soon as he spotted her.

A red-blooded American male, he couldn't miss the flowing head of sun-kissed hair draped down a back that narrowed to her tiny waist, not quite reaching the rounded hips that swayed their way across the quadrangle. So mesmerized by the beauty strolling away from him, his buddy elbowed him muttering something about *pick his tongue up off the floor.*

Feeling sorry for himself after missing his chance to catch up to her, not that he'd had a clue what he would have said had he actually intercepted her, he'd moped around campus all afternoon. Seated in his last class of the day, he'd almost swallowed his tongue when he looked up and who should walk through the door? His redhead. Having only seen her from behind, he was totally blown away by her sparkling green eyes and bright grin.

The downside, because life had a way of always tossing a downside into the mix, only inches behind her, a tall, what most women would probably call hunk, said something that made her laugh. Craig still remembered the odd sense of irritation that had kicked in and made him want to growl at the guy. Instead, he casually kept an eye on her as she took a seat beside Mr. Hunk. She'd laughed, giggled, blushed, and a few times they'd leaned into each other to whisper something no one else was meant to hear. In other words, his mind-numbing redhead was taken.

All semester he'd watched the two arrive and leave together, and debated if he should just step in and ask her out anyway. The problem with that was two-fold. First, he knew both his mother and grandmother would come down hard on him for poaching another man's girl. Second, one thing he never wanted was to be looked upon as being a chip off his father's philandering block. Not that Craig was attached to any one lady to be considered a philanderer, but he wasn't a man-ho either, so he did nothing. Not even towards the end of the school year when watching her and Mr. Hunk walking up the street and Craig realized all along she'd been living only two doors down from the townhouse he and his roomies shared.

Even though he hated to admit it, he'd kept an eye out for her on campus right up until the day he graduated, but had never had the chance to run into her again. Until today he hadn't even known her full name, and had no idea if she'd broken up with Mr. Hunk or married him. He couldn't resist quickly glancing in the direction of her left hand. *No ring*.

How silly was it of him that he wanted to do a fist pump. A lot of years had passed since college and Spanish Lit class and the old house on Elm Street. Other than she was probably the most beautiful woman he'd ever seen, he knew very little about her. Something he had every intention of correcting.

"I hate to be the bearer of bad news." Devlin cleared his throat. "But you're trespassing."

Kate's eyes rounded as wide as the owl now peering down at them. "I am n…, I mean…" Her back stiffened and a fire reappeared in her eyes. "I'm sure once the owners realize they have a protected species nesting on their property they won't object to me hanging around until I can get some decent photos."

"Perhaps, but I'm afraid, now that I know you're here without my clients' permission, I have to either wait for you to leave, or call the police."

She seemed to grow an extra inch as her spine grew stiffer. "No need. I can leave." In sharp, jerky motions, she reached for the sleeping bag at her feet.

"Here." Craig hurried forward. "Let me help you gather your things."

"I don't need any help, Mr. Baron."

Sucking in a deep wince, he wasn't sure his name had ever sounded so dirty before. "Please call me Craig."

One brow rose as those fiery green eyes glared at him. "That won't be necessary."

Her arms laden with the few things she'd gathered together, she spun around on her heel and lifted her chin at Dev. "Tell your clients that they can expect to be hearing from the Fish and Game Commission soon." Not waiting for his response, she stormed out.

At the sound of an engine roaring to life, he realized she'd parked her car behind the barn and out of the line of sight of the road. "She seemed pretty ticked off."

Dev nodded.

"Did we have to throw her out?"

His cousin slowly turned his head to face Craig and shot a steely glare at him that made the one Kate had given him look down right friendly. "You may not have to answer to anyone, but I have a license I'd like to keep. Heaven forbid she did something to burn the place down or compromise the property in any way."

"She's not like that."

"And you know this how?"

For a moment he considered telling his cousin it was just a hunch, but what was the point of that. "We went to college together. She's a nice girl." Or was.

"Funny, she didn't say anything about knowing you."

Craig shrugged. "That might be because she didn't

know I was alive back then."

"That's got to be a first." Amusement danced in Devlin's eyes. "Still, if the owners found out I knew she was here, I'd be selling designer knockoffs on a street corner."

"Yeah. I get it. But I meant what I said earlier. Let's finish looking around, then I want to know everything about the property from the mineral rights, to any other protected species that might interfere with my plans."

Dev nodded. "At least there's one thing you can be sure of."

"What's that?"

"There won't be any deed restrictions prohibiting building a movie studio."

And that was exactly why he'd chosen to look in the vicinity of Houston and not closer to his home in Austin. Not only did he spend way more time at the ranch than he did at his townhouse, but government red tape was never fun. When it came to Austin, the city had mastered the art of permit complications. On the other hand, this not so little property held great potential, wouldn't have a homeowners' association, nor neighbors to grumble to the city about the inconvenience of rows of parked cars or bright lights turning nights into days. Too bad it didn't come with a town in the backyard and the pretty redhead with a fiery temper.

"Do I want to know why you're slamming those poor pots about as if they were a weapon of mass destruction and you were out to annihilate the world?"

Kate bit down on her back teeth and turned to her roommate. "They threw me out."

"Who did?" Eyes narrowed, Joan took a step forward and lifted her fisted hands onto her hips. "Do I need to call Tiny to go beat someone up?"

Kate didn't know if she should laugh, roll her eyes, or apologize to the now boiling pot of water. "We haven't seen

Tiny in years."

"That's only because he had to do time for that little misunderstanding."

"Misunderstanding?" This time Kate almost laughed at her friend's Pollyanna approach to the transgressions of others. To this day Kate had no idea what Tiny's real name was or how the six foot four hefty young man with a shaved head, earring, tattoos, and leather accessories ever got such an inappropriate nickname. "He went away for grand theft auto."

"His brother told me Tiny had no idea the car was stolen. Besides, he should be out by now, and you know he always had a soft spot for you."

Soft spot was an understatement. At first, the sight of their next-door neighbor scared the bejesus out of her, but it hadn't taken long to learn that under the rough and tough façade, Tiny was a very tenderhearted and thoughtful guy. Quite the gentleman. If he saw her pull into the driveway, he'd be over in a shot to help with groceries, miscellaneous packages, or simply pull her door open for her. The first time he'd done that, she'd been reaching for her purse in the passenger seat when her door flew open and she almost landed on Tiny's military grade boots.

"So," Joan smiled, "who are we siccing Tiny on?"

"We're not siccing him on anyone. I went back to the barn this afternoon, prepared to camp out all night if necessary, waiting for the bird to leave the nest so I can get some photos. See if she's tagged and if there are eggs in the nest."

"And if there are? What exactly do you think you can do about it?"

"I don't need to do anything about it." Technically, the bird was in the wild in a relatively untouched area and she could just stay away and hope for the best. After all, most owls didn't have a lot of natural predators. But it was the soon to be baby owls that had her more concerned. They were prime pickings for coyotes and other feral animals roaming about those parts.

"Then maybe you should stop taking it out on that poor

pan." Joan's sideways grin made her laugh.

Taking in a deep breath, she lowered the flame under the pot of water and more quietly set the frying pan on the stove. "Now I just need to figure out how to get back to the barn and check out the nest."

"I know saving the environment is your job, but in this case, I think the babies will probably be fine without your intervention."

"I know." She scraped the raw hamburger meat into the pan and began dicing onions. "But you know I can't help it. Someone has to stand up for the animals."

"And you do it so beautifully." Joan grinned and sniffed at the browning meat and seasonings. "Though I will admit, it's kind of nice when you're ticked off and start cooking. I love your spaghetti."

"I hope you love my lasagna too because that's what I'm making."

"Yum. Even better." Joan grabbed a handful of almonds from a nearby bowl. "Now that it's safe to stand near you with a knife in your hand, what are you going to do next?"

"I'm not sure. I might reach out to Craig."

"Craig?"

Kate nodded. "The man who told me to leave is Craig Baron's cousin."

Almost choking on the almond she foolishly swallowed almost whole, Joan's eyes bugged out as she stared up at Kate. "Tall, dark, and rolling in dough Craig Baron?"

Kate nodded again.

"The one with all those cute brothers?"

Again, Kate dipped her chin in affirmation.

"Wow." Joan dropped onto the nearby stool and leaned on the island. "Hunky Craig Baron from your college lit class. Who'd have thunk?"

Joan had hit the nail on the head. Who'd have thunk she'd ever run into Craig Baron again. Actually, who'd have thought she'd ever have a chance to knock Craig on his butt.

"You're smiling." Joan paused, a chocolate covered almond halfway to her mouth. "What aren't you telling me?"

Mixing the ground beef and jar of sauce, she lowered the flame to simmer, then turned to her long-time friend. "You remember those self-defense classes we took last year?"

Joan nodded. "Every black and blue too."

"Well," her grin widened, "they work."

"I don't understand." Joan's face scrunched in confusion.

"He startled me and I sort of took him out."

The whites of Joan's eyes circled wide around her dark brown eyes. "You're kidding?"

"Nope." She adjusted the lid on the sauce pan to keep it from boiling over. "I might have overreacted a tad, but he caught me by surprise."

"Well, good on you! I hope we never have to find out if I learned anything."

The two of them chuckled for no good reason. But Joan was right about one thing, monitoring a nesting owl was not her responsibility. On the other hand, if everyone walked away from a chance to ensure a successful breeding season, there would be a lot more endangered and extinct species in the world. Now all she had to figure out was what was she going to do next, and just how close and personal with Craig Baron did she really want to get? Though if she had to choose between Craig and the owls, Mr. Bossy Baron didn't stand a chance.

CHAPTER FOUR

The last week had been grueling. Even though it wasn't his preferred method of running the business, he kept tabs on the two productions running with video calls. After only a few more days with every available hour spent scouring options for sale within a fifty-mile radius, it had become clear that nothing appealed to him the way the Martin property did. The owl was simply going to have to find someplace else to roost.

"You have that strained look on your face again. You must be thinking." Devlin came in and dropped a stack of papers on the desk beside his cousin. "It took a little fancy footwork and fast talking, but once I got the executor on our side, he was able to convince the heirs that waiting wasn't going to get them a better offer and it was in their best interest to take the money and run. Though *I'm* not convinced this is the right move for you."

If he were to tell the truth, Craig wasn't totally sure that buying the Martin place—owl and all—was the best move he'd ever made, but nothing else fit his plans as well. He'd already reached out to a few of his cousins in the construction business and gotten guesstimates of what something of the scope he had in mind could cost. While it was a great deal of money, the potential for return was hard to walk away from. Especially considering some of the projects he had in the works. But more so, this would be a stellar opportunity to offer the diva what no one else could—a film produced exclusively in the state of Texas. It didn't hurt any that a blockbuster hit would do wonders to skyrocket his soon-to-be studio to the top of the in-demand filming locations from the get-go.

Sitting across from him, Dev dropped his ankle across his knee and leaned back in the chair. "You worried about the owl?"

"No."

"You realize if there are eggs in that nest you won't be able to do construction on the barn."

"We can start on the other buildings until I can arrange to have it moved."

Dev's eyes rounded. "If that woman gets Fish and Game involved, you'll need an act of God to get the bird's nest moved."

"Maybe." If there was one thing he'd learned in life, it was that the old adage *where there's a will, there's a way* held a great deal of truth. Hand in hand with *it's not what you know but who you know* and he wasn't even a little worried about one little owl messing with his plans. Once again his mind kicked over to visions of Kate Donovan. Several times over the last few days, Craig had picked up his phone and debated reaching out to her. It hadn't been very hard to track down her phone number. Years ago, when someone had tried to frame and blackmail Mitch for an imaginary indiscretion, the Governor had turned to a former navy Seal. Luke 'Brooklyn' Chapman had proven to be better at his job than the Governor had bragged and he and Craig had hit it off. To this day they remained friends. After Craig's call, it had taken Brooklyn all of thirty minutes to track down Kate's private cell number. Another twenty-four hours and Craig had a complete dossier on her. Not that there was much to report, but he knew when and where she was born, where she got her MBA, who she worked for up until she started her own firm, and that she was considered one of the best environmental consultants in the business for expert court room testimony. Not only was she top of the game for saving animals on land, sea or air, she was pretty darn good at putting away the bad guys destroying animal and human habitats, so to speak. He just hoped it didn't come down to him being one of the bad guys.

The report also mentioned she'd never been married, though there was no mention of what happened to Mr. College Hunk or anyone in between. All of which had nothing to do with his current real estate plans. Any tinge of doubt he might have had fell by the wayside knowing the deal was moving forward. Bird or no bird, this was the perfect acreage to eventually establish one more Baron enterprise. "Where there's a will, there's a way."

"That works best on a needlepoint pillow."

"Go ahead and tell that to our grandfather."

Dev shrugged. "No, thank you."

It took Craig several minutes to study the contract in front of him before initialing the few requests the family had. Since Texas used promulgated forms, filling in the blanks had made the process easier. The one time he'd been involved in a deal in New York it had driven him nuts that the contracts had to be drawn up by attorneys, and the fees to go with it were high enough to give him permanent heartburn. "We'd better give the title company the go-ahead if we're going to close in less than a week."

Dev nodded. "Already have."

There was no hiding the grin that tugged at his cheeks. His cousin was good at what he did. There wasn't another realtor on the planet Craig would have trusted to negotiate this deal. The family who had ignored their granddad's land for decades had an over-inflated opinion of the value and Dev had been just the man for the job of convincing them otherwise. He initialed the corrections to the estate's name as well as moving the closing date up from Friday to Thursday. "And we're all done."

"You'd have made one hell of a real estate investor." Dev flashed a cheeky grin. "You have no idea how hard it is to convince most investors that in a fight for a lowball offer, no contingencies are the best weapon."

"Low ball? Whose side are you on?"

"Why, my client of course." Dev dropped his feet to the floor and leaned forward, resting his forearms on his knees. "You've got five days to figure out this bird thing, because on day six there will be a herd of contractors rolling in to start turning this wasteland into your dream."

His cousin was right about one thing, if he saw this deal all the way through, Baron Studio Productions would be more than a dream, it would be a little heaven on earth. A few more strokes of the pen and the execution date was in place. There was no backing out now. Handing the pages to his cousin, he pushed to his feet. "If you'll excuse me. I have a phone call to make."

Judging by the knowing sparkle in Dev's eyes, his cousin knew who the phone call was to. Grinning like the cat who'd swallowed the proverbial canary, Dev held the pages up. "I'll get this scanned and off to the executor and title company."

"Thanks, man." Another few seconds and Craig was alone. Cell phone to his ear, he listened to the number he was calling ring once, twice, three times, and pondering what message he would leave when voicemail kicked in, he was surprised at the velvety voice on the other end.

"Hello."

"Kate?"

"Yes."

He could hear the question in her voice. "It's Craig Baron."

"Oh." The simple and curt one word response had him preferring the confusion to irritation.

"It was nice running into you the other day." He waited for her to say something, but greeted by only silence, he hurried on. "I was hoping I could convince you to join me for lunch, or maybe a cup of coffee if you prefer?"

Silence lingered uncomfortably. He came within seconds of rambling on about wanting to help save whatever animal she was invested in when she finally spoke up. "I guess I can do that."

Since he had no idea if she was talking lunch or coffee, he decided to do what he'd done his whole life. When given an inch, take a mile. "Great. As it turns out, my day just cleared up and I'm free for lunch today. How about I pick you up in an hour?"

An hour! Kate's mouth went totally dry. Swallowing a jar of peanut butter would have been easier than peeling her tongue away from the roof of her mouth, never mind producing a coherent sentence. "Uhm." Could she be ready in an hour? Did she have something she needed to do? Absurdly, all rational sense seemed to have leaked from her brain. She couldn't remember if she was coming or going. "I, uh, think so." Could she sound any more lame?

"Wonderful. Are you still living on Mossvine Lane?"

"Yes. I am." How the heck did he know that? Suddenly this little impromptu invite felt…creepy.

"Glad to know Google actually gets some things right."

"Oh." Somehow that seemed to make sense. After all, hadn't she come home from the escapade at the barn and Googled Craig James Baron herself? "Then I'll see you in an hour."

"An hour," he repeated before adding a polite "see you later" and hanging up.

She was still staring at her cell phone screen when a co-worker came up to her. "Is it ticking?"

"Excuse me?" Kate shifted her gaze to Debra.

"Your phone. You're staring at the thing like it's a ticking time bomb about to explode."

Maybe that was it. Maybe having lunch with one of the most eligible bachelors in the state, one she'd had a full-blown crush on for the better part of her four years in college, was nothing more than a disaster waiting to happen? After all, what did she have in common with Texas Royalty?

"Earth to Kate." Deb waved a hand at her.

"Sorry. Got a lot on my mind."

"The turtle nests or the barn owl?"

"Huh?" Kate blinked, quickly processing what her friend had said. "Oh. Neither. Well, maybe the owl."

"Well, that's clear as mud. Talk to the Fish and Game guy yet?"

Kate nodded. "Yeah. He's going to let me know when he can meet me at the barn."

"I know I've said this before, but I still think…what's his name again?"

"Craig."

"The Fish and Game guy?"

"Oh, sorry. Ted."

Deb dipped her chin in a single curt move. "Right. I still

think Ted is more interested in you than the owl."

Now her brain was clearing up. "And I told you before, that's ridiculous. We worked together once on a case with Dr. Carter and it was strictly professional. He doesn't have a thing for me any more than Peg Carter does."

"How many times did he invite you out to grab a bite to eat?" Now Deb stood tapping her foot.

"Is it a crime to catch a bite to eat with a colleague?"

"No."

"See? And we never did catch up for lunch, so there."

Deb sprouted a huge grin. "I rest my case."

"Now that makes no sense." Maybe the dazed one was Deb, not her.

"He wants that lunch and is willing to drive out to the middle of nowhere over a protected, but not endangered, bird because you are the one who called him." Before Kate could open her mouth, Deb held her hand up. "No need to argue. We'll just wait and see who's right."

On a deep sigh, Kate shook her head. "Whatever. In the meantime, I'm heading out for lunch. Not sure when I'll be back."

"That sounds ominous."

"Not quite, just catching up with an old college classmate."

"Male or female?" Deb was grinning again.

"If you must know, male."

"Ooh. As in, old flame?"

"As in, never noticed I was alive, but now we're having lunch."

Deep lines formed between Deb's brows. "That makes no sense."

"No. But it is what it is." Before Deb could come back at her, Kate grabbed her purse and flung it over her shoulder. "Have to run. We'll talk more later."

Deb called after her, "I'm going to hold you to that!"

And that almost scared Kate as much as lunching with a member of the most powerful family in the state of Texas. Almost.

CHAPTER FIVE

Not since the premiere of his first feature film had Craig been this nervous. It simply made no sense that a woman he hadn't seen in well over a decade, and barely knew, was making him sweat like an acne-covered teen on prom night.

To his surprise, rather than live in an easy low-maintenance condo or town home close to downtown like most young singles, Kate was planted in the heart of Houston suburbia. In a lovely older established neighborhood filled with what would have once been called starter homes. Unlike the surrounding brick homes, this house was cement sideboard. A pale, not quite blue, not quite gray house, with dark shutters and flower boxes under the windows filled with red, purple, and orange blooms gave him instant insight into Kate Donovan.

Not only was she determined to save the planet and its inhabitants, she wasn't afraid to make it a more beautiful place at the same time. A well-manicured lawn and a Pavestone walkway led him to the dark red door with a lion head brass knocker. As he stood rooted to the front porch, debating whether to ring the bell or use the knocker, the door flew open. "Hi."

"Hi." He glanced away to the video door bell and Kate nodded.

"It alerted me as soon as you pulled up to the curb." Tugging at a purse hanging over her shoulder, she took a step forward. "Ready?"

He bobbed his head and took a step back, giving her room to walk beside him. For a split second he considered extending his arm but decided it might be a bit much for a casual lunch invitation. "Do you prefer fish or beef?"

"Not sure I have a preference."

As soon as the words left his mouth, it occurred to him that given her line of work saving the animals and the planet, maybe she was vegan or vegetarian. Thankfully, he wasn't going to have to scramble looking for an appropriate place to eat. He had a list of favorites and his best bet was picking something that offered traditional American fare, a little of this and that, and he knew just the place.

"I must admit," Kate buckled her seatbelt and turned to face him, "this was a bit of a surprise."

"A good one, I hope." He pulled away from the curb.

It took her longer to respond than he would have liked, but finally she bobbed her head. "I think so."

He was going to have to do his best to make sure that his phone call and invitation shifted from 'I think so' into the most definitely a pleasant surprise category. "I'm glad. I have been staring at your phone number for days, debating whether or not to call."

Her brows buckled and she tugged at the strap across her chest as she shifted in her seat. "Which begs the question, how did you get my cell phone?" The words were barely out of her mouth when she held her hand up. "Never mind. Some days I forget how far-reaching Google can be."

At this particular moment, he didn't think it wise to explain about Brooklyn. If this led to anything more than lunch, he'd have to find a way, but for now, he'd be willing to live with what his Catholic friends called a sin of omission. Only a few minutes in average traffic and he was down the freeway to one of his favorite eateries.

"So what made you call?" Her question was addressed to him, but her gaze was on the traffic ahead.

He wasn't quite sure how to answer. Or maybe what to answer.

"You said you had my number for days. Why did you finally call?" Her more in depth question told him she must have mistaken his silence for confusion.

"Frankly, after what happened with my cousin, I was afraid you might hang up on me. Or worse."

"Worse?"

He shrugged. "One thing I learned early in life is never underestimate a smart woman. Especially if you've pissed her off."

"Oh, I detect a good story hidden in there somewhere." The corners of her lips tipped up in just a hint of amusement.

He'd forgotten how beautiful that smile was, but the same as it had in college, the warmth and sweetness of her grin punched him hard in the gut. For the life of him, he couldn't remember having such a visceral reaction to a woman's smile. "I remember that smile. From Spanish—"

"Lit class." The grin widened.

For a moment he tore his gaze away from the road ahead and took in the twinkle in her eyes. "I didn't think you remembered."

"How does a mere mortal forget when she's in class with Texas royalty."

Oh, how he hated when the media referred to the Baron clan as royalty. "I was hoping it had more to do with my boyish good looks and southern charm."

Kate tipped her head back and laughed from deep in her throat. The sound made his smile widen and his fingers tighten on the steering wheel. There was no doubt in his mind he was going to love every minute of finally getting to know his redheaded classmate. "You certainly had Senora DeLeon charmed."

Truth was, he had most of his professors charmed. Except for Doc Benson, his statistics professor, who had a real thing against legacy families. Or maybe just Barons. "Whatever happened to that friend of yours?"

"Joan?"

He shook his head. "The guy who sat near you in class."

"Oh," her smile softened, "Steve. We were going to save the world together."

"Were?"

"You know how it is in school. Everyone is starry-eyed with dreams of grandeur. After college Steve moved on to Woodshull and now he's somewhere in the South Pacific."

"A modern Jaques Cousteau."

"Something like that." Her smile remained sincere. Whatever happened, there wasn't any bad blood. "I like the idea of saving my little corner of the planet."

And wasn't he glad to hear that. Well, except for the corner of his barn with that darned owl. Exiting the freeway, he followed the service road a short distance and pulled into the parking lot. "Here we are. Hope you like it."

Her smile slipped just slightly as she blinked several times before looking to him. "I've heard nice things about this place."

"You've never tried it?"

She shook her head.

"Then you're in for a treat." He hurried around the front of the car and reached the passenger side in time to help her out. It was a ridiculously old-fashioned thing to do, helping a woman out of a parked car, but it was as ingrained in him by his mom and grandparents as it was to breathe in and out.

"Mr. Baron." Mario, one of the three brothers who owned the restaurant, greeted Craig. "How wonderful to see you."

"It's been too long. How are Tony and Joe?"

"Fine. Fine." Mario grabbed two menus. "Your regular table?"

Craig nodded, and gently placing his hand on the small of Kate's back, guided her to the far corner by the large picture window.

A few more pleasantries were shared, and promising the waitress would be right over, Mario hurried away.

"This is a surprise." Kate looked out the window onto the large array of trees and shrubs. "It's like being in the woods."

"It is a bit unexpected. It's not as large a section of land as the view implies, but back when their parents started the restaurant, Houston wasn't quite so crowded. A lot of developers have tried to buy this back lot and the brothers refuse to sell."

"I don't blame them. It's lovely."

"The food is pretty good too. Most of the recipes go back generations, and the meat rub is their dad's secret recipe. If you like a good steak, I can't recommend the rib eye enough."

She bobbed her head and smiled. "I'm a carnivore through and through."

When the waitress came by, Craig ordered the shrimp croustades for an appetizer, the beet salad, and a rib eye for both him and Kate.

Once they were alone, Craig took a quick sip of water. "So how did you wind up going from Spanish Literature to saving the planet?"

Still smiling, she shrugged one shoulder. "Probably the same way you went from Spanish Lit to making movies."

"That was easy. I spent one year working on the Spanish Riviera for Baron hotels and decided very quickly the hotel business was not for me. There was a movie company filming some cheap short and they needed extras. I was there and available, so I mulled around as requested. The one-off chance clip turned into another offer on another film, and after a year the business had gotten under my skin."

"Talk about perfect timing."

"Most definitely. So what's your story?" Polite chit-chat was part of the status quo of getting to know a girl. He had all the tell me about yourself prompts down pat, but today, this was probably the first time he really wanted to know the answers. He truly wanted to know, who is Kate Donovan?

Kate needed a sip of water to calm her nerves. There was no explanation for why she felt like a schoolgirl on her first date. Craig Baron may have just brought her to one of the most expensive five-star restaurants in North Houston, but he was still just a man. Flesh and blood. Probably put his pants on one leg at a time like all men.

"Tell me, why save the animals?"

"Honestly." She set her glass down on the table and leaned forward a little. "I've always been a saver. As a kid I would bring home squirrels that had fallen out of their nests, or rescue baby bunnies from my predator cats."

Leaning back in his seat, smiling at her, he nodded. "That I can picture."

She smiled back at him. "My degree is actually in psychology, but when I graduated, the thought of five more years of grad school before I could use the degree was daunting. Instead, I took a job with a friend of my father's firm."

"Conservationist?"

"Nope. Handbag Factory. I was the president's executive assistant."

"Not a good fit?"

That smile of his kept threatening to steal her breath.

"Not at all. I hated working behind a desk, but I thought that's just what adulting meant."

"I hear a *but* coming."

"I really hated that first job, but I didn't know what was missing. Then a few of us went on vacation in Hawaii. We came across a beach during turtle hatching season. We camped out at the edge of the beach a few days."

"As in tent and campfires or…"

"It would have been trespassing to sleep there—"

"Like at the Martin's barn."

The urge to sigh and roll her eyes was almost stronger than her social skills. Whether the retort was arrogance from a lifetime of affluence and privilege or simply a red flag on the jerk meter, she wasn't sure. "As I was saying, we showed up every morning early and stayed until we couldn't hold our eyes open. Then one morning we saw movement by one of the markers. Sure enough, the hatching had begun."

"Must have been fascinating." The tone of superiority had slipped away, replaced by a sincere smile and signs of what could be a really nice guy.

Just what she needed. Jeckyll and Hyde. "It was,

except," she swallowed hard, "it broke my heart seeing how many birds swooped in and captured the little creatures making their way to the ocean."

"Couldn't you help?" The way he frowned, she was sure he felt her same distress.

"We could try to shoo the birds away, but those beaches are sacred. We couldn't really walk around for fear of damaging a nest, and it's illegal to touch the sea turtles in any way—even to help them into the water."

"But that didn't matter. You were hooked." Now he was grinning like a cat with canary feathers between his teeth.

"Pretty much. I did some volunteer work for about a year, then decided to go back for my masters in animal conservation, and then went to work for a preservation company to learn the ropes."

"Did it work?"

"Too well." She looked around as if someone from her old job might be eating beside them and listening. "After a few years I had moved up the ranks enough to be given some prime assignments. And then things got sticky."

One brow shot up on Craig's forehead but he remained quiet.

"We'd done some testing of ground water and shoreline waste near a tire factory. There were some nasty accusations from nearby residents and we were the neutral third party called in to determine if the health issues were connected to the factory."

"And were they?"

"Absolutely. They were taking enough short cuts to crumble the Golden Gate Bridge."

Craig sucked in a breath, his mouth remaining briefly in a sour pucker. So maybe all the money and power did give way to a nice guy underneath.

"But the real kicker was the fat envelope stuffed with hundred-dollar bills in my glove compartment."

Shifting in his seat, Craig winced. "Oh, hell."

"Exactly." She hadn't told anyone all the details before and had no idea why of all people, Craig Baron made her want to talk. "Needless to say, the bribes went very high up the ladder and my not wanting to *play nice* almost killed my career before it started."

"Corporate shenanigans can be rough."

"Don't I know it." She waited for the waitress to set their food dishes down and walk away before continuing to speak. "Let's just say, the whole thing left a very sour taste in my mouth and opened my eyes to the evils of big business—and their money. I got out of that one by the hair of my chinny chin chin. Walked away and never looked back."

"And started your own firm." It wasn't a question, but he looked really pleased.

Oddly, she felt like puffing out her chest at the unspoken praise. "And have done quite well too."

"I know." He cut into his meal. "A lot of good people have been taken down under circumstances like that. You should be proud of yourself."

"What I'm mostly proud of is that the SOBs went to jail, the water got cleaned up, and the factory sold to owners willing to follow the rules."

"Good for you. It's not easy to take on corporate America and win." His gaze studied her with an intensity she hadn't expected. "What are you doing tomorrow?"

"I have some reports I need to work on. Next week is a busy week and I often use the weekends to catch up."

"Come to the ranch with me?"

"Excuse me?"

"My family is sponsoring a fundraiser at the ranch for a new charity my grandparents are helping my neighbor get off the ground. The last one they held did so well they're making it a quarterly event for now. There will be kids, a petting zoo, games, prizes. You'll have fun. I promise."

Every fiber of her being told her that playing in the ultra-rich world of the Barons of Texas was not a good idea, but she wouldn't be where she was now if she weren't willing to take at least a few risks. Now the question was just how risky a mess was she getting into?

CHAPTER SIX

Craig felt like one of his sisters. He'd actually changed his slacks twice and his shirt three times. While his sisters were known for having their entire closet strewn on the bed while they changed three, four, or more times for a date, whatever he put on first had always been what he wore. Not today. At first he'd put on khakis but decided jeans at the ranch made more sense. Then he put on a light blue polo shirt, but for some reason he felt like a Smurf. The beige shirt came out, but now he looked all washed out. Finally, he settled for an ordinary navy blue crewneck top with a breast pocket. Tempted to change one more time, his common sense kicked in and forced him to get going before Kate arrived and found him still upstairs messing with his wardrobe.

"We're so glad you're able to join us for the fun today." At the bottom of the stairs, his grandmother kissed him on the cheek on her way past him to the kitchen. "I need to check with Hazel on a few last-minute details. You might want to see if Mitch and Chase need any help in the stables."

Craig glanced at his watch and down the foyer to the front door.

His grandmother's face lit up. "Waiting for someone?"

"As a matter of fact—"

Lila Baron's brows dipped into a sharp V. "And why are you not picking her up? We taught you better than that."

"Yes, ma'am. But she insisted on driving up from Houston on her own. I didn't think it right to be pushy." What he didn't want to tell his grandmother was that some women just felt safer in control of their transportation. Not that he was sure that's why Kate insisted she could drive herself, but he didn't want to dwell on it in his own mind anymore than he wanted to explain what he didn't quite understand—like why he was as nervous as a cat in a room full of rockers—to his grandmother.

She dipped her chin, the frown slipping away. "I think I understand. Very well." Another kiss on his cheek and she was gone.

"Why, don't you look smashing." Siobhan came practically bouncing out of the kitchen, a cupcake in one hand and a cookie in the other.

"I see you're dieting again," he teased.

Still hanging on tightly to Hazel's freshly baked snack food, his little sister flung her arms around him and kissed his cheek. "Hardy, har, har." Taking a step back, she held out her arms to either side of her and struck a model pose. "As if this perfection needed to diet."

Knowing she couldn't do anything about it with her hands full, he reached forward and tussled her hair the way he'd done when she was a little kid. It was hard to see his little sister all grown up. She had always been a cute kid and she'd blossomed into a real knock out. He still wasn't sure he liked it. Soon there'd be love, then marriage, and eventually kids for Siobhan, but no matter, he would always see her as the baby of the family.

The doorbell rang and Jeeves appeared instantly in the doorway. Craig held up his hand. "I've got it."

The family butler bobbed his head and did a perfect military turn on one heel. Siobhan simply stared up at him with a gleeful grin. "Do I need to leave you and your, uhm, guest, alone?"

Craig rolled his eyes heavenward and shaking his head, hurried to the front door. Swinging the door open wide, he could not help but smile at the beauty in the doorway. The lady knew how to wear a pair of jeans.

In a blue button-down shirt and a cowboy hat on her head, she held out a small bouquet of fresh flowers. "These are for your grandmother."

Circling around her big brother, Siobhan reached for the

flowers. "She is going to love these. Why don't you to go ahead and do whatever it is you're going to do, and I'll take these into the kitchen for some water."

Maybe his baby sister wasn't quite as grown-up as he thought. Right now she looked exactly like the little girl in braids teasing him and his siblings about their dates. Not that this was an official date, but Siobhan's youthful playfulness was shining bright.

The flowers gripped firmly in one hand, Siobhan extended her other hand. "Sorry, I can't resist teasing this guy. I'm Siobhan, it's a pleasure to meet you."

The nervous switch at the corners of Kate's mouth widened into a relaxed smile. "Kate Donovan, lovely to meet you."

Siobhan released her grip, and smiling, took a step in retreat. "I'll meet y'all outside in just a bit."

Craig turned to face Kate. "Shall we do as the brat said?"

"She didn't seem so bratty to me."

"She never has been. I guess I need to stop saying that. It's just hard to accept that she's grown-up." Closing the front door behind her, he gestured towards the main living room. "Shall we?"

Kate nodded and fell into step beside him. "I think it's kind of sweet."

"Sweet?"

"Yeah. I know you were both teasing each other, but it was obvious to me that it was all done with a great deal of love."

Having crossed the living room, he opened the back door onto the massive veranda that spread from one side of the house to the other. "That we do have plenty of. She really is a great kid." He slammed his eyes shut, and then quickly opened them again. "I mean, she's a great lady."

Patting his arm, Kate followed him down the back steps. "There there, that wasn't so hard, was it?"

"Harder than you think."

"Oh my." At the bottom of the back steps, Kate scanned what was usually open grassland but now overflowed with tents, and booths, and plastic table cloth covered tables scattered from one side to another. "That has to be the biggest bounce house I have ever seen."

"We're expecting a lot of people."

"Apparently." Her gaze darting from one spot to another as they walked, she looked both intrigued and surprised blended with a dab of bewildered.

"Hey, want to give it a test run?" Manning the corn hole area, his sister Paige extended her arms and waved the bean bags clutched in both hands. "First round is free."

"Is that your marketing pitch?" Craig rolled his eyes.

"Don't knock it. There's a reason loss leaders have been key in growth marketing." She rolled her eyes right back at him, spun about to face Kate and shifting the bean bags to one hand, extended her other hand. "Since my big brother seems to have forgotten his manners, I'm Paige Baron."

"Nice to meet you. Kate Donovan."

"Despite what this lug thinks, it really is a good marketing strategy." Paige held out the bean bags. "Go ahead. Show him how it's done."

Kate's eyes sparkled, her smile widened, and accepting the bean bags, she glanced over her shoulder at him. "Watch and learn."

Taking her time, she studied the wooden boards and swung her arm forward and back several times before letting the bag sail across the way and slide right through the first hole.

"Lucky shot," Craig called to her. A few more minutes and three more bags made their way into the holes without a skip or slide. Holes in one.

Paige applauded loudly. "I think I'm going to like you. Not everyone can best my win-at-all-cost brother."

Brushing her hands together, Kate moved to his side. "Your turn."

"Later. Grams said they might need extra hands in the barn." He nudged Kate toward the barn and gave his sister a fast wave as they walked away. He'd barely crossed the threshold when his brother Mitch appeared with a calf on a rope following behind him.

"Oh." Kate eyes flickered with delight. "A baby cow."

His lips curled over his teeth, Mitch bit back a smile.

Craig quickly introduced the two. Kate's head snapped around in his direction, he could almost feel her excitement at the prospect of being this close to a real *baby cow*. "Can I pet him?"

"Sure." Mitch stopped in front of her. "We're on our way to the petting zoo."

Kate stretched her hand forth under the animal's nose the way one might when testing a dog's temperament.

"Go ahead and scratch behind his jaw. He will love you forever," Mitch instructed before turning to his brother. "Grams and I thought the kids would get a kick out of Ginger's foal. You two want to bring her over?"

Kate's head bobbed so fast, he was surprised it didn't snap off. "I don't know that I've ever seen a pony at a petting zoo."

"That's because they can be little shits." Mitch sighed. "But Ginger's girl has a good temperament. I think all will be well."

"Oh, this is going to be fun." Kate clapped her hands together.

If only Craig could be the one to make her smile so merrily. He'd have to work on that.

When Kate accepted the invite to the little fundraiser, none of what she'd found was what she'd imagined. She hadn't really spent a great deal of social time, who was she kidding, any time at all with the ultra wealthy, and as soon as she'd turned onto the road that led to the driveway that led to the most beautiful massive white house she'd ever seen, her palms began to sweat and a nest of fledgling birds began flapping around in her stomach. She was most likely seriously very much in over her head. And yet, inside, everyone was as casual and friendly as if she'd walked into a sorority house. From the house to the outdoor games to the barn, every interaction with the Baron family surprised her.

Understanding why people used the expression cow eyes, she gave the little calf one last scratch under her chin and followed Craig to the horse's stall. When he pulled the door open to expose a large reddish horse and the cutest little mirrored image of her, she almost squealed with delight. "Isn't she pretty."

"Yes. They both are."

Craig attached some contraption to the small horse's head with a rope to help lead her by. The walk to the petting zoo area was a short one. Briefly, they made the rounds to the different animals. There were little pigs that were beyond precious when they squealed, the baby cow and horse, a few rabbits, goats, and the sweetest looking lambs. "Are these all from the ranch?"

"No. We're limited to cattle and a few horses. The rest are on loan."

As they walked along from booth to booth, Kate was quickly educated in the size of the Baron clan. So far every single booth was manned by a sibling or a cousin. The odd thing was, by the time she was done meeting everybody, she could tell which siblings were from which clan. Craig and his family all had similar features with varying shades of chestnut hair. On the other hand, his cousin Devlin and his sister Leah along with other siblings, Rachel, Cooper and Claire all had sandy blond hair and mostly green eyes.

From what she could tell as the crowds grew, the Baron family were either manning the booths, or spending the money. The ticket price to play corn hole was only a dollar, but Craig and his cousin Porter had each slapped $100 bill on the counter. She made a good living, but dropping $100 bill on a carnival game was a bit outside her budget.

For their next stop they wandered over to the horseshoes. Instead of his cousin Porter, it was Craig and another cousin, Porter's brother Colton, competing, and once again a hundred dollars was at stake. After a few tosses she'd finally understood the expression close only counts in horseshoes. She had no idea which one of the two men was the more competitive, but when Craig's cousin made the game-winning toss, he crowed like a preening peacock.

"You pick next." Craig stopped walking and waited for Kate's response.

She took a minute to survey the grounds and truthfully she was always the one who held the handbags, balloons, and snacks while her friends rode the roller coaster or played the arcade games. Judging by the obvious competitive history that ran in the Baron family, she wasn't all that sure she wanted to play against Craig or any of his family. "Too bad y'all didn't put up a bowling alley. That I could probably do."

"You like to bowl?"

"Used to love it. In high school my friends and I would hit the alley every Sunday afternoon. I wasn't headed to the pros, but I really enjoyed it. And for the most part, kept the ball out of the gutter, too." Still scanning the horizon, she wasn't sure what to choose, and then she saw it. A dunking booth. Whenever she'd seen a watery tank in a movie or TV show, she'd thought it looked like fun. Maybe it was a deep down need to get out her frustrations with the crazy rules in the world, but she really wanted to try. And who knows, maybe her corn hole tossing skills would roll over into ball pitching skills. "Is that a relative in the dunking booth?"

Craig followed the direction her hand was pointing and slowly his eyes lit up and his smile brightened. "Oh, yeah. That's Adam. I can't believe someone talked my straight laced actuary cousin into sitting in the dunking booth." He turned back to face her. "You any good?"

She shrugged. "Don't know. I've never tried."

"If you're half as good at the dunking booth as you are with corn hole, this is going to be epic."

Quickly linking his arm with hers, he practically dragged her across the way to where his cousin sat on the bench over a still pool of water. "Hundred dollars for the fundraiser and another hundred to your favorite charity if you can drop Adam into the water."

She had a feeling this was a little more of that friendly,

loving, teasing, or at least she hoped so. Craig paid his sister Eve, who was collecting the money and handing out the softballs. Kate had thought the balls would be something designed to be a little heavier, but at least with the larger ball she stood a better chance of hitting the bull's-eye.

Holding the ball in her right hand to get a feel for it, she concentrated on the metal tab. In school, the PE coaches always told the students whether playing tennis or baseball or field hockey to keep their eyes on the ball. Hopefully, the same held true for the dunking booth tab. Staring intently, she pressed her lips together, raised the ball high behind her and let it fly. Even though she'd missed it by a mile, Craig had grinned and cheered. "Great throw. You got this."

Clearly, she wasn't as convinced of her skill sets as he was. Shifting her weight onto her right leg, once again she stared down the bull's-eye, refused to blink, and heaved the ball across the booth. Another miss.

"That's okay. You're just finding your groove." Craig smiled at her. "You've got this."

She wished she had as much confidence in herself as he seemed to have. At least she had three more balls to toss. Lord, how embarrassed was she going to be to have missed the tank five times by a mile.

Leaning over the counter, Eve curled her finger at Kate and lowered her voice. "You might want to shift a little to your right. You seem to have a bit of a hook."

"A hook." She nodded. "Got it. Thanks."

Eve glanced over her shoulder at her cousin and then turning back to Kate, flashed a bright smile. "You got this."

She really wished everyone would stop saying that. Moving a few short steps to her right, she tossed the ball slightly in the air and caught it a couple of times, pretending to get a feel for the weapon of choice, but really praying for inspiration, or a sudden gift of a professional pitching arm. Muttering to herself, *here goes nothing*, she once again let the ball fly from her fingertips.

Only this time, the ball appeared to be sailing straight toward the bull's-eye. Curving slightly to the left, she found herself leaning with the ball, her hands clasped as if in prayer, when the large white orb connected with the metal tab. A bell clanged. The boards dropped out from under Craig's cousin and the cocky grin slid from Adam's face at the same time he collapsed into the water.

"I did it!" Gushing with excitement at her unexpected accomplishment, she spun around and threw her arms around Craig. Repeating her triumphant cry, "I really did it!"

Slowly, Craig's arms wrapped around her waist as he muttered softly near her ear, "Yes. You. Did."

CHAPTER SEVEN

Kate had no idea why she'd bothered going to bed early last night. She might as well have sat up watching infomercials. Maybe then the boredom would have knocked her out. Instead she rolled out of bed at the first sign of morning light and spent the next hour sipping coffee and staring into her closet.

Yesterday had been an absolute blast. She'd had so much fun. At first watching the Barons playing—their competitive streak was a hoot. Then getting involved herself. By the end of the night, she'd gotten much better at corn hole as well as horseshoes and almost peed in her pants from laughing when the adults went into the bounce house after the event was officially shut down.

Despite the sheer smell of money coming from every corner of the magnificent house and splendid grounds, this family laughed, and played, and teased and even fought, just like anyone else. As nervous as she'd felt the first little while in the massive home, it hadn't taken her long to feel as though she'd known this family her whole life.

"You're smiling." A mug in hand, Joan sat down on the edge of the bed and blew on her morning brew.

"Am I?" She knew she was. Even if she was completely stumped as to what to wear this afternoon, she couldn't help but grin at the memories of last night that replayed in her mind. Especially that unexpected hug after she'd dunked Adam, and the warmth of Craig's breath whispering in her ear that sent tingles down her spine all the way to her toes.

"Okay, now you're downright beaming. If you hadn't been home before me last night, I'd say there'd been some hanky-panky making you smile."

"Of course not." She shook her head. Even if she had attended class with Craig a million years ago, she barely knew the guy. Heck, they weren't even dating. Yet. Maybe.

"Now you're frowning? What the heck is going on?"

"I don't know what to wear." That wasn't the whole truth, but it was definitely enough.

"Where are you going?"

"I don't know."

Perfectly arched brows buckled at the bridge of Joan's nose. "What do you mean you don't know?"

She fingered her black capris. Not as casual as shorts, not as warm as long pants. "He wouldn't say."

"He? *Who* he?"

"Craig." Maybe a denim skirt would be a good choice.

"Craig?" Deep-set lines between her roommate's brows remained, then suddenly her eyes rounded wide. "Wait a minute. So now, you're dating the guy who's messing with your owls?"

"Not exactly dating, really. And he isn't doing anything with the owls." *Yet.* She pulled out a simple pale blue sleeveless dress from the closet and held it against her. "Do you think this is a good choice for an afternoon invitation?"

Joan glanced at the dress. "If you're going to high tea, yeah. If you're going to the zoo, not so much. And you're skipping over the good stuff. How did you wind up going from an afternoon fundraiser to a secret rendezvous?"

"You've been reading too many romance novels. It's not a rendezvous and it's certainly not secret. I simply have no idea where we're going. All he said is wear something comfortable."

"Well, that doesn't usually mean a dress."

"But it *is* comfortable."

"For you, yes. But I doubt that's what he had in mind."

Kate sighed. "Maybe I'll think better after I get some more coffee."

"Some food wouldn't hurt." Joan pushed to her feet and placed her free hand on her friend's back. "This isn't rocket science. Your new jeans fit you like a glove and it will look great with that pale green top, the one that darkens your eyes."

"You think?" She fingered the short sleeve blouse hanging in her closet.

"Yes, I think. And as soon as I get some food in you, you're going to tell me all about this Baron that has turned your very competent brain into Swiss cheese."

"There's nothing to tell." And if her friend believed that, Kate had a bridge in Brooklyn for sale really cheap.

Second-guessing himself was not something Craig did often, but ever since saying goodbye to Kate last night, he'd been doing just that. Why had he made such a big deal about keeping his plans a secret? What if she didn't like his idea? What if she was expecting something fancier? More creative, or romantic? Not that she had any reason to expect romance from him, but still. And there he was, second-guessing his second-guesses.

Keys in hand, he sucked in a deep breath and reached for the front door just as his grandmother came up behind him.

"Another date?" She smiled.

For a second he considered telling her it wasn't a date, and even though he hadn't phrased it to Kate that way, he knew full well this was very much a date. "Sort of."

"Sort of?" Her brows arched high. "Maybe things would work out better if you were more sure."

And wasn't that part of his morning debate. All morning. "Yes, ma'am. I know it's a date, I'm just not so sure she does."

"Ah." The woman's smile widened. "Don't worry so much. I bet she knows too."

"Love you, Grams." He leaned over and kissed her on the cheek.

Lila Baron giggled like a schoolgirl and patted her grandson lightly on the arm. "Go win her over."

Grams was still standing in the doorway as he drove off. That woman was unconditional love personified. He hated to think what life would be like when she or the Governor were no longer around. Turning his head from side to side, he shook away those thoughts. Instead, he picked up the phone as he turned onto the main road. "Hey, Fred. Are we all set?"

"Yes, sir, Mr. Baron. Just what you asked for. We're ready when you are."

"Great. We'll be there in about an hour."

"We'll be waiting."

Call disconnected, he raised the volume on the stereo searching for something to distract him from third and fourth guessing himself. The drive into town went by faster than he'd expected. First thing he noticed, Kate had added a new basket of seasonal flowers on the front porch steps. The woman really had a touch with all things living, whether plant or animal. A vision of her giggling at the calf licking her face brought a smile to his own.

As the other day, the door flung open before he could knock. "Hi. I—"

"Saw me pull up," he finished for her.

Her head bobbed, and hands gently at her side, she did a semi turn. "Is this okay? Or should I change into something else?"

"Perfect." As far as he was concerned, everything about her was perfect. From her strappy sandals, to the jeans that hugged her curves, to the sweet smile, and sparkling green eyes. Absolutely perfect.

"I'll freely admit, I'm not so sure about today." Kate folded her hands on her lap.

"Why is that?"

"Getting in a car when you don't know where you're going with someone you've only recently met is everything every girl's mother warned her against, not to mention the start of many a good or bad horror film."

That made Craig laugh. She had a point about the horror films.

"No offense," she added.

"None taken. Besides," he glanced in her direction and flashed his best aren't I cute smile, "I've never produced a horror film."

Her head tipped and she leaned against the door. "How'd you go from making films to building a studio? I mean, there are a lot of producers who don't own their own studios?"

"Correct, but there are a lot who do."

She nodded. "So you're just following the crowd?"

From the way her brows buckled, it was clear she already knew him well enough to question that concept. He smiled and shook his head. "Nope. It's practical. A lot of the good perks for filmmakers are coming from cities in out-of-the-way places—for Texas—most popular right now is Canada. Frankly, the flying back and forth to film sites is losing its charm."

"I can understand that."

"Besides, I've got a big project upcoming and having wide open space options to film in one place instead of moving crew all over for different locations would be a huge money saver, not to mention remove the logistics nightmare of coordinating all of it."

"Won't it take a long time to build a studio?"

He nodded. "Everything I plan to do, yes. Initial construction for immediate filming of smaller projects—not really. Getting from buying the rights to a movie to actually start filming takes a lot longer than you would think. Mostly because there are so many moving parts, so many different parties involved, and usually they don't like each other, or talk to each other, so everything takes ten times longer than in the ordinary business world."

"Doesn't that sound fun?" Even though she was smiling at him, her tone dripped with sarcasm.

"You know," his grin broadened, "it really is. The art of making the deal is often more fun than the process or the finished product."

"I like it when a project is done and I get to see the fruits of our efforts."

The car slowed and he pulled into the parking lot of the bowling alley. As casually as he could muster, he glanced at her to see her reaction. Not till he pulled into a parking space in the nearly empty lot did she glance up and see the sign.

"We're going bowling?" From her tone he couldn't tell if that was a good or bad thing.

"Unless you'd rather not?" Fifth guessing kicked in.

She spun around in her seat, her eyes sparkling and her smile wide enough to touch her ears. "I love bowling."

"You mentioned that." Suppressing a delighted grin at her enthusiastic response, he undid his seatbelt and circled the hood, reaching her door before she was fully out of the car.

On her feet, she blinked at him, and then her grin dimmed to a soft smile. "You remembered."

He bobbed his head and hoped his cheeks weren't burning bright red from the delightful way she looked at him.

As they entered the bowling alley, the normal hum of balls rolling, people chatting, and the clattering of falling pins was blatantly missing.

Kate stopped short at the front desk, scanning the surroundings. "Don't people bowl anymore?"

"Sure they do." No point in mentioning that he'd bought out the alley for the afternoon. It had taken a little doing, something about league games, but one of the perks of being a Baron was not counting pennies.

A young man who looked like a giant on the elevated center check in desk smiled down at them. "Renting shoes? Or have your own?"

Craig's first instinct had been to pop over to the pro shop and buy them each a pair of shoes, but common sense reminded him that most of the bowling population rented shoes and none to his knowledge had dropped dead from cooties. "What size do you wear?"

At her response, the clerk handed her a pair of fairly new-looking shoes. "Do you need socks too?"

"You rent socks?" Craig couldn't hide the incredulity in his voice.

The kid laughed. "No, sir. We sell those."

"We'll take two pairs."

Bowling had changed a lot since the last time he'd graced an alley. Everything was electronic. No papers, no need for scorekeepers, no arguing over how many points a turn took, and definitely no cheating.

"You ready to get your butt whipped?" Kate stood at the edge of the alley, her feet lined up with the dots on the wood planks. Concentrating for a moment, the ball in front of her, she took three long strides, her arm swinging back and the ball hit the wood deck and rolled straight, curving just in time to strike the sweet spot by the head pin. "Strike!"

Normally, that much enthusiasm would only succeed in egging on his competitive streak, but it looked so darn cute on her all he could do was grin.

It had been ages since he'd bowled, but surely it was like riding a bike, you never forget. Lining up center lane, he held up the ball and stared down the lane. It had really been a long time. He reminded himself to mind his steps, the direction of this thumb, and before he could make a move Kate giggled behind him.

"Need some pointers?" she called out.

He didn't say a word, just turned and over his shoulder delivered the Baron death glare. "Now you're on."

For the next couple of hours they were neck in neck from one game to another. She'd won the first game. He'd called that practice. Then he'd won the second and now they were on the best two out of three. He couldn't remember the last time he'd had so much fun. The competition had been more playful as they laughed and slapped high-fives, and teased, and snacked on decadently greasy foods. Competition with his family had always been high pitched, tense, and often involved grumbles and even a little cussing. This was perfect.

More than once he'd had to step back and resist the urge to pull her into his arms and offer a congratulatory kiss.

"Oh drat." Kate looked at her watch. "How did it get to be so late?"

"They do say time flies when you're having fun."

Leaning over to untie her shoes, she glanced up at him. "This really was fun. Thank you so much."

A few more minutes and they were in the car and

heading back to her house.

"I'd almost forgotten how much I enjoyed bowling." Kate pulled her hair back and stuck a clip to hold it off her neck. "I wish I didn't need to finish that darn report or we could have played longer."

"We'll do it again."

"I'll hold you to that."

"I'm counting on it." He took a chance and reached across the console to give her hand a quick squeeze and was rewarded with an even wider smile than a moment ago. "Will the report take long?"

"I hope not. It's a pre-trial assessment. A neighborhood association is suing an old paint factory for failure to complete the agreed upon clean up in order to avoid federal prosecution. The corporation hired me to rubber stamp the report that said the site was cleaned up and safe for the neighborhood."

"Uh oh."

"Yep. Apparently, no one told them I don't do rubber stamps. I do my job and I don't think they're going to like my opinion."

"Ouch."

"That's one word for it." She twisted in her seat to face him. "I don't want to think about that till I have to. We got sidetracked earlier. Have you found a place for your studio?"

"Absolutely. The Martin place is going to be perfect."

"What?"

CHAPTER EIGHT

The Martin place was not what Kate expected.

"That location is perfect."

"But the owl?"

"Is a bird. This is business."

Suddenly Mr. Nice Guy reverted to Mr. Rich Guy in a heartbeat. "You can't undergo construction with a protected species nesting on the location. Your studio will wreak havoc on the owl's new habitat."

"Do we know he's nesting or just hanging out in a convenient spot?"

She should have known this would happen. "Nesting or resting doesn't really matter. The issue is habitat. We have got to protect nature's habitats."

"Agreed."

"What?" Again, not what she'd expected. Was he trying to confuse her on purpose?

"We need to protect the environment. Heaven knows my family is at the front of the line for defending the underprivileged, disadvantaged, and for all I know soon to be extinct. But..."

Of course there was a but. Crossing her arms, she couldn't wait to hear what self-satisfying spiel he was going to spew.

"For all we know the owl has already moved on to another barn and another abandoned nest."

She had to admit, he might have a point, but she doubted it. "No matter what careful plans you might try to make to leave as little of a footprint on the land as possible, it is still going to be more of an impact on nature than a working ranch. It would be easier for you to simply keep looking for a spot that isn't providing a natural habitat to wildlife, especially protected or endangered species."

"Too late. We closed on the deal Thursday. It's all mine. Lock, stock, and old barn."

"And owl." She couldn't help the bitter tone that came out. "You should probably know the Fish and Game agent is meeting me there tomorrow."

Craig's one brow rose higher than the other as he cast a sideways glance in her direction. "I see. Don't they need to notify landowners?"

"I'm sure the Martin family has been notified. Texas doesn't exactly record property sales in a timely fashion."

"Tell me about it," he sighed. "Still, it's private property and as Devlin mentioned, coming on the property without permission is trespassing."

"Going to call the police on us?"

"Of course not."

"Well, there's that." She tugged on her seatbelt and shifted to look at him again. "So what *are* you going to do?"

"For starters, not jump to conclusions. We may have a little time. After all, a project of the size I have in mind doesn't exactly happen overnight. There needs to be architectural drawings. Engineer reports. Permit filings. Of course, my cousin Porter will be general contractor so I don't need to put out a call for contractor bids."

"Is that wise?" Her irritation at his disregard for the environment was beginning to ebb as she realized that none of the things he was talking about were going to come together quickly. Not that it mattered if the owls intended to make his barn their new—and permanent—home. Still, she wasn't in the real estate business, but even she knew it was not smart to do any construction without at least three bids.

When he turned to face her, she expected a scathing glare. Instead, she was faced with a smile and soft chuckle. "Normally, I would be the first to say not wise at all, but we Barons live by a multitude of codes. One of which is family sticks together. We support each other, we comfort each other, and we never cheat. Porter will come in at a reasonable price, and more importantly, he'll have my back.

Everything will be done right. Maybe better."

She couldn't decide if he was putting family before profit or counting on family to make him a nice profit. But her gut told her if push came to shove, and Craig had to choose between the bird and his construction schedule, that the bird wouldn't stand a chance.

The minute he'd informed her of his choice of the Martin property and her only response was the single word *what*, Craig knew he was in trouble. What he didn't know was how to get out of it. Business was business, but right now he considered if walking away from the real estate project might not be the right thing to do.

"We're meeting at noon." Kate leaned back in the seat. "Ted has worked with me on other projects. Since I was never able to get close enough for good photos, he needs to check if there are eggs or hatchlings in the nest and if the adult owl is tagged."

"Tagged?"

"Yes. As policy, environmentalists tag and weigh all hatchlings, then follow them throughout their lives. Migration patterns, etc."

"Makes sense. So if there are no eggs or baby birds and mama has already been tagged, then we're in the clear?"

"There's still the adult bird to consider. Construction havoc, the noise, the vibrations, the general chaos can stress a bird."

"You're kidding." He couldn't hold back the chuckle. "I can show those birds a thing or two about stress."

Kate rolled her eyes and sighed. "You know I'm not kidding."

"Yeah, I'm afraid I do. But you can't blame a guy for trying." Now all he had to do was figure out a way to make his bankers, his production company, Kate, and the birds all happy. "How well do you know this guy from Fish and Game?"

"So so. Why?"

"Is he a rule follower or does he think outside the box?"

From the stretch of silence, he could only assume the question either stumped her or had her thinking.

"He definitely is a rule follower. Most government agency employees are, but I have no idea about the outside the box thing."

"I see." He might have to do a little research of his own. There was no doubt that Brooklyn was one helluva detective, but there was little doubt in Craig's mind that owls were not in the former Navy Seal's skill set. Even though Craig had excellent staff, including people perfectly capable of doing a little research, in this case, he wanted to keep the whole protected species and the potential problems that could come with that, close to his breast. At least until he had a little more data. "We'll probably both have answers by tomorrow."

She nodded. "Yes. I'll fill you in."

"Fill me in?" Momentarily taking his gaze off the road, he tossed a glance in her direction. "What time is he coming?"

"I don't know. In the morning. He's supposed to give me a heads up tonight." She glanced at her wrist. "I suspect it will be first thing."

"I'm expecting to meet with the engineer tomorrow. Maybe the architect too. I suspect we'll have our answers sooner than later."

"More family?"

"Excuse me?" This time he kept his eyes on the road.

"The architect and engineer."

"Oh." He smiled. "Engineer, yes. Architect, no. I do have a cousin who is an architect, but Rachel specializes in restoration."

"If anything needs restoring it's that barn."

"Perhaps, but it's not going to be restored, it's going to be converted and there's no keeping the integrity of the structure when it's going to be used for a soundstage."

"Sound," Kate muttered and shifted forward in her seat, but didn't say another word.

Craig had no idea how this was going to straighten out. All he could do was start praying that owl was on his way to Mexico. Despite his telling Kate that things in this biz moved slowly, he had every intention of fast-tracking every aspect of this studio as much as he could. He could only hope the bird was not going to throw a wrench into his schedule.

The remainder of the ride to her house was made in awkward silence with minimal conversation. He'd tried circling back to the bowling game. That had at least brought a smile to Kate's lips, but the gleam in her eyes from earlier had yet to make another appearance. Sticking to neutral topics like yesterday's fundraiser, the petting zoo, and slew of adults making fools of themselves in the bounce house was helpful, but that blasted bird and its potential nest hung over them like a dark cloud. Knots deep in his gut were twisting about like wet rope and it had nothing to do with the scope of the studio project and everything to do with the prospect of losing the attention of one Miss Kate Donovan. The feeling wasn't much different than how he'd felt back in college every day watching her come and go with that smiling macho man.

Pulling into her driveway he was torn between being thankful for a few hours to figure out his next move, and forlorn at having to say goodnight. He certainly hoped not goodbye.

"Thank you for a fun day." Her smile was sincere, but lacking the brilliance from earlier in the day.

"Thank you for being a good sport. I had a really great time too." He hated to bring it up, but there was no way to avoid the elephant in the car with them. "I'll see you tomorrow?"

She nodded. "I'll text you when I know what time Ted will be there."

"Sounds like a plan."

Once again she nodded. Her smile had grown weaker and seemed more forced than sincere. He wouldn't have been surprised if her face hurt from the effort. Her hand on the door handle, he hurried around but by the time he reached the passenger side she'd already climbed out of the car.

The stiff smile still plastered on her pretty face, she tightened her grip on her purse and took a short step in retreat. "Tomorrow."

This time, he nodded in silence. Leaning against the car, he kept his gaze on her as she made her way up the walkway, placed the key in the lock, and with a final wave, slid into her home and closed the door.

Pushing away from the fender and slowly walking around to the driver side, he blew out a deep sigh. Somehow, he couldn't help but think he'd stand a better chance winning Kate over if his only competition had been Mr. College Hunk. Cute and endangered owls might just best him, and he didn't like that thought one bit.

CHAPTER NINE

"You're up awfully early." Twirling the wayward strands of long blonde hair and tying it into a sloppy bun on the top of her head, Joan stifled a yawn.

Kate didn't dare tell her roommate it was more a matter of being up really late. She had tried to crawl into bed and get some sleep, but after tossing and turning for close to an hour, she sat up with a bad book in hopes it would put her to sleep. No such luck. Another hour and she opted to clean out the junk drawer she'd been promising to straighten for the better part of the last year. Or was it two? Whatever, the drawer was incredibly neat and organized, she'd swallowed a gallon or two of coffee, and now she had to face Ted and Craig, and most likely kiss a blooming relationship goodbye.

"Coffee?" Joan held up the half-empty pot.

"No thanks. If I have any more I'm going to be twitching all the way to the barn."

"That's right." Joan poured herself a cup. "The owl."

At least today she wasn't going to need an hour to figure out her wardrobe. It was a work day. Jeans, boots, and layers, thanks to the ever-changing Texas weather; cold as an Alaskan morning one minute and roasting like a Thanksgiving turkey the next.

"For someone who was grinning like the Cheshire Cat yesterday, you don't look very happy this morning. Maybe you should go back to bed for a couple of hours."

The idea sounded wonderful—if she could sleep. Glancing at her wristwatch, even if she could, there wasn't enough time. Ted had texted her last night that he planned to be at the barn between nine and ten this morning. "Not enough sleep, too much coffee, and the most interesting and exciting man I've met in years is starting to look less and less like Prince Charming and more and more like an ordinary toad."

"Ouch." Joan popped an English muffin into the toaster and turned to face Kate. "That bad, huh?"

Kate shrugged. "The almighty dollar for the win."

"I'm sorry." Joan blinked. "Translation please?"

"What am I always up against?"

"Corporate America." The toaster popped and Joan turned away. "Or stupid people."

"Craig isn't stupid, but typical big business, he's putting profits ahead of the owl."

"And that's a surprise why? The Barons are not only a social, corporate and political powerhouse, they are the closest thing to royalty in the state of Texas. You have to know their bank accounts are blossoming for a reason."

That was not what she wanted to hear.

"Maybe," Joan reached out and patted Kate's shoulder, "you should wait and see how this show plays out before you lose any more sleep."

"Maybe." Clutching the mug handle, she pushed away from the table. To her caffeine addled brain, the chair legs scraping across the floor sounded like fingernails on a chalkboard. The way she calculated the situation, she had just enough time to finish her lukewarm coffee, shower, dress, and hit the parking lot often referred to as a freeway. "I'll let you know how it goes."

"For what it's worth, I'm hoping he turns out to be a real prince." Joan flashed a cheesy grin. "With a brother for me."

One thing was sure, if Craig Baron wasn't too good to be true, there were enough single men in that family to make a village of women very happy.

Despite a lack of sleep and over abundance of coffee, Kate was showered, dressed, and making great time on the bumpy road to the barn. At this rate, she was probably going to beat both Craig and Ted to the Martin place.

Though, she supposed now it was the Baron property. Or Baron Studios. She actually shook her head at that. Who wanted a big business in the middle of rural Texas anyhow. The owl and its new habitat was the main concern, but who knew how many other animals all this construction was going to unsettle.

Already moving alongside the broken-down fence that surrounded the property, as she turned the bend that came just before the driveway, she could see a slew of cars parked by the barn in the distance. She had no idea why she thought a little past eight thirty in the morning was going to be too early for big business. Rolling her neck in a useless effort to ease the increasing stress making itself at home in every cell in her body, she took in a deep breath and blew it out ever so slowly. All this activity was most likely already stressing that poor bird. "Men."

Resisting the urge to slam her car door and stomp over to where Craig and another guy hovered over the hood of a massive pickup truck, she straightened her shoulders, grabbed her binoculars and camera, and slowly marched across the gravel drive. "Morning, gentlemen."

It took Craig a moment longer to stop tapping at the papers on the hood of the truck and look up. A smile touched his lips and darn that man if all the fire she'd been breathing for hours didn't wash away.

"Your friend has been here for a while."

"Friend?" *Duh.* "You mean Ted?"

Craig nodded. "I took the liberty of showing him these preliminary sketches that the architect drew up."

"Morning," the man she assumed had drawn the sketches nodded at her.

"Sorry." Craig straightened and took a step back from the truck. "Kate Donovan, you remember my cousin, Porter Baron."

She nodded and at the last minute decided there was no need to be rude and forced a smile. "Nice to see you again."

"The pleasure is all mine." Apparently, there wasn't a Baron yet who hadn't inherited the charming gene.

Craig cleared his throat and actually nudged his cousin

back a step. That was almost enough to make her laugh.

"I should go look for Ted." She cast a glance in the direction of the barn.

"He's already been in the barn." Craig straightened. "Last I saw he was walking the perimeter heading toward the main house. If you can wait a minute, I'll go with you."

Dressed in jeans and chambray shirt, another man came walking out of the barn. Even with the cowboy hat shading his eyes, she didn't need a family portrait to know he was another Baron, but his name had slipped her mind. "You may not be as crazy as I thought."

Craig looked from her to the latest guest to the party and she raised her hand at him. "I'll go find Ted. I'll be fine."

"No. There could be snakes. Give me one second."

She held out one foot. "Wore my boots today."

"Still." Craig pressed his lips tightly together and gave her a pleading stare.

"No need." Porter pointed in the distance. "Here comes the fed."

Right now the way both his cousins were practically drooling at Kate, Craig wasn't sure if he wanted to scoop her up and whiz her away, or slug Porter and Cooper.

His still grinning cousin removed his hat and extended his hand. "Cooper Baron. Nice to meet see you again."

"Likewise." Kate shook his hand and looked from Porter to Cooper then to Craig. "If you're both cousins, then neither of you is the architect? Or did I misunderstand?"

"You remembered correctly. The architect was busy this morning. We visited last week and he drew up the initial drawings. I brought them so we could get some preliminary plans confirmed while your friend is checking out the owl. Porter is the general contractor."

The first cousin she'd met nodded and smiled at her again.

"That's right." She bobbed her head. "You did mention Porter before." That made the cousin's grin grow a little wider.

Craig waved a thumb at his other cousin. "And this guy is the engineer."

"The engineer who is surprised as all get out." Cooper waved a thumb at the barn in the distance. "I don't think it's going to be as extensive a project as I had feared from your preliminary update. I don't think permits will be an issue either."

At that moment, Ted came within hearing distance. "We throwing a party?"

Earlier when Craig had introduced himself as the property owner, he'd been the only one there so Ted had not met the two Baron cousins. The men shook hands, exchanged some curt but polite words, and then turned their attention to Kate. He really wished he could step in front of her and yell *back off* without looking like a complete fool. Or worse.

"Learn anything?" she asked.

Ted bobbed his head. "The owl is tagged."

Craig knew better than to speak up until all information was given, so he gave a short nod and waited.

"I spotted the tag with my binoculars. Couldn't get close enough to retrieve the data. We'd need to see where she's been this last year. In order to do that we have to catch her."

Again, Craig merely nodded. So far his mind was thinking, *good, catch her, read her tags, and let her go to someone else's property.*

"Since I spooked her, I was able to get close enough to the nest."

And this was the moment Craig had been waiting for with less than bated breath.

"She's got eggs."

Not what he wanted to hear.

"We'll have to wait for them to hatch. Then we'll want to weigh them, tag them, and..." Ted shrugged at Kate. "Well, you know the routine."

Kate's head bobbed an affirmative response, but her

gaze was off at the barn. "So no construction near the barn?"

The agent blew out a heavy sigh and Craig tried not to wince. He did not need more bad news coming.

"That owl is only one of your problems."

"What do you mean?" This time Craig refrained from keeping silent.

"I walked the property and checked some of your hollow trees."

Doing his best to maintain a stoic expression, Craig's hands fisted in his pockets.

"You've got Black Striped Texas Bats. Hollow trees are some of their favorite hibernating spots and from the looks of it, even though it's spring, I found at least two trees with bats still in hibernation."

All of this was more than Craig cared to deal with. Taking a second to process the possibilities, he glanced in Kate's direction. His pretty redhead was nibbling on one corner of her lower lip. That could not be a good sign.

"All of this means what exactly?" Cooper asked.

"We're going to have to have a team come in and check all possible habitats for more bats."

"Team?" Craig didn't like the sound of that.

"We're rather short-handed in general, and I'm stretched more than thin." Ted cast a glance in Kate's direction and offered his first hint of a smile. One that told Craig if not for her, this little tete-a-tete would be at the bottom of Ted's to-do list sometime next spring. "As it is, as much as I wish I could fit this into my schedule, I'm going to have to hand this little finding off to one of the probies. Most likely, there will be an army of grad students available to search and mark the habitats. Once we have that straightened out, you may or may not be able to do some construction away from all the nests."

"Birds or bats?" Porter asked.

Ted shrugged. "Both."

Cooper turned to Craig. "This isn't looking good."

That was exactly what Craig was thinking. If they didn't break ground soon, there was no way he was going to be able to pitch his studio to the Austin diva with deep pockets and the movie he'd been itching to get a piece of. For a brief moment, he wondered how much would the fines set him back for ignoring everyone and moving forward anyhow, but immediately, he discarded the potential public relations nightmare from his options. Like it or not, he was going to have to figure out a solution to make his spreadsheet—and Kate—happy. His gaze surveyed the land that extended as far as his eye could see. Hands still fisted in his pockets, he blew out a soft sigh. Fish and Game, his college crush, bats, birds, and bankers. Once again his gaze drifted to Kate. Somehow he had to make this work, because losing Kate again, and over a bird and a bat, was not an option.

CHAPTER TEN

Kate kept an eye on Craig the entire time Ted was talking. None of the Barons looked overjoyed, but she knew this would happen. Knew how it works when big business collides with Mother Nature. The only problem is this was the first time she wished she weren't on the other side. She really wanted to find a way to make everyone happy, but truth was, when it came to conservation, compromises needed to be made on the side of big business because endangered animals had no other options.

"I need to get going." Ted took a step back, extended his hand to gently pat Kate on the arm. "I'll be in touch with an update."

She nodded. "Thanks." From where she stood she could see Craig biting down hard on his back teeth. She couldn't blame him, his very expensive plans were about to blow up in front of him.

Ted waved at the other men, and their eyes followed him to his vehicle. No one said a word until the engine turned and the dust disappeared onto the main road.

"Now what?" Porter asked.

"We hit the drawing board. Plans need to be finalized. Permits have to be applied for. Decisions made. None of that will happen overnight."

Both cousins nodded and Craig's calm approach took a little of the nervous edge off of Kate's concerns that Craig would blow a gasket.

"You know," Porter tapped at the papers spread out on the hood, "we're going to be ready long before the Fish and Game Commission gets around to dealing with these bats."

Craig pressed his lips tightly together, sucked in a deep breath, glanced down at the rough draft of his plans, and looked back to his cousins. "With the grace of God, maybe the eggs will hatch and the bats will leave sooner than later."

She hated to be the bearer of bad news, but she didn't have much choice. "You do realize once the eggs hatch, it will be weeks, possibly months, before the birds will leave the nest?"

Craig nodded. "Sometimes, you simply have to play the odds."

Somehow, that didn't make her feel any better. "Show me what you have planned."

Craig's head snapped up. His eyes wide and focused on her, for a minute she thought he was going to say no. "Come around here."

Circling the massive ranch truck, she sidled up beside him and immediately recognized her mistake. Arm brushing up against his was a much bigger distraction than she needed. Taking a short step to the side, she bumped into one of the cousins. "Sorry."

Cooper smiled. "No worries."

Craig skewered his cousin with an intense glare before clearing his throat and tapping at the papers. "All of these are existing structures according to the survey that was done. They all have to be examined in detail to determine the extent of any structural issues before we proceed with remodeling."

"Wow." She hadn't realized how many buildings there were or how large the property was.

A slow smile teased at the corner of Craig's lips. "Told you it was perfect. This," he pointed to the main house set back across the driveway from the barn, "will be our offices." One by one he moved from building to building explaining his intentions. "Multiple sound stages, converting the existing large farm equipment buildings into storage for cameras and lights."

"How much room do you need for lights?"

That had Craig chuckling. "We're not talking table

lamps. These are massive lights designed to make a set, whether indoor or outdoor, look like broad daylight."

"Really?" She turned her attention to the storage garages on the paper, and then squinting, tried to spot the actual buildings in the distance.

"Really. The lights are huge, hot, expensive, and on wheels. Not having to spend $5k to rent the suckers for days on end will be a huge budget savings."

"Oh." Five thousand dollars seemed like a lot of money, but she supposed movie equipment might fall into the same category as home ownership. Cheaper than renting.

"It's all about money, budget, and timing. If we're shooting a scene on the beach in Malibu with a massive hill in the background, when the sun goes down, filming can't stop. So the lights go on. You can get around it a little with close-ups, but the folks who have their back to the hill need those lights, otherwise it looks like they're in front of a black curtain."

"So you're saying not everything I see on screen is real."

Craig let out a deep in this throat chuckle. "Not even close. And those lights wreak havoc with wildlife. Every owl, deer, and bird on the face of the planet will misconstrue the lights for daylight."

"So, you've dealt with wildlife before?"

"You mean like the time we did a bonfire scene on the beach and a family of raccoons went berserk?"

"Oh, dear."

"Well. Not in a bad way. The baby raccoons were totally freaked so mama raccoon kept squawking and making noise trying to deal with the babies. Pretty much, when filming outdoors with bright lights, audio becomes a nightmare. Every creature comes alive and audio picks up every animal but can't capture the actor's dialogue. You hear crickets not the actors. It just adds to the joys of moviemaking." His phone sounded, he glanced down at his phone and raised a finger. "I have to take this."

She nodded and watched him walk away from the car as he spoke to whoever was on the other end, then looked back to the plans.

"I guess there's an awful lot of lights to store if he's going to need all those massive garages."

Porter nodded. "Every set needs trailers for makeup, the stars, if they're filming away from plumbing, Porta Potties, generators. All of which need to be kept somewhere when not in use."

"I didn't realize." She looked at the drawings again. No wonder Craig wanted so much land. "You seem to know a lot about the movie business."

"Not really." Porter shook his head. "Just repeated what Craig told me and the architect."

"Of course." Still, she was completely floored by the proposed undertaking.

"Who the heck holds a major gala on a Monday night?" Craig blew out a sigh and dropped his phone into his breast pocket, then turned to Kate. "I don't suppose you like black-tie affairs?"

Craig had forgotten that he promised his grandfather he would represent the Barons at tonight's political gala for the up-and-coming protégés for both US and State representatives. When he'd agreed ages ago, it hadn't occurred to him that he'd be up to his eyeballs in a major project *and* saving owls and bats.

"Is that a trick question?" Kate tipped her head at him.

"I'm afraid not. I have to go to a political gala tonight. It sort of slipped my mind and I don't have a date. These things tend to be rather boring, but stag they just drag on."

"Political gala?" Her brows dipped into a pensive V. "As in the ten thousand dollars a plate dinner downtown political gala?"

"The one and only."

Her jaw dropped and her eyes widened and then a slow sassy grin took over her face. "Do I get to talk to anyone I want?"

Now Craig was wondering what had he just gotten

himself into. The last thing he needed was to create a scene for his family. Especially for Mitch. "Depends on who you want to talk to."

"There's some legislation on the table to help our jobs protecting the sea turtles and a few other at risk animals here in Texas. It's not perfect, but it's a start. That is if we can get it out of discussion and up for a vote. The political bigwigs have been dodging my calls for months. I wouldn't mind cornering them over champagne and deviled eggs."

He didn't want to tell her the odds of being served deviled eggs were slim to none, but he wouldn't mind seeing a few of those stuffed shirts cornered by a gorgeous redhead on a mission. "Sure. Why not."

Both her hands slapped together and then brushed quickly with enthusiasm. "This is going to be seriously cool."

There was no escaping the laughter that bubbled inside him from her gleeful response. "If you say so."

"What time are you picking me up?" The way her eyes darted about, he could almost see the wheels turning in that busy little mind.

If a night out with a bunch of stuffed shirt politicians and dressed up like a penguin was all it took to put that smile on her face, he'd help her corner every single person who had been avoiding her. "Cocktail hour starts at seven. If I pick you up at 6:30 that should get us there at a fashionably appropriate hour."

She flicked her wrist to look at her watch. "I can do that."

Since it was only a little after ten in the morning, he wondered if he was asking too much of her, dropping this at the last minute. "If you don't have time, I'm sure we can corner the right people some other time."

"No." She shook her head vehemently. "This will be perfect, but I have a lot to do in a short amount of time if I'm going to be fit to hob knob with Houston's rich and famous."

As far as he was concerned, she was fit to hob knob just the way she was.

CHAPTER ELEVEN

"How do I look?" Kate spun around in place for her roommate.

Joan nodded approvingly. "Every man in the place is going to be picking his tongue up off the floor. I wish I could wear that shade of green as well as you do."

Her hands carefully skipped down her sides. "I thought about the black dress. You know, classic and all that, but I thought it might be too boring."

"There's nothing boring about this outfit. If you're really worried, in a darker room it might look black."

"No. I like the green shimmer. I was afraid the neckline might be too low." She spun around to look in the full-length mirror for the millionth time since getting home from the hairdressers.

"It's perfect."

When she'd spotted this dress on a mannequin at her favorite department store, she'd fallen in love. The cap sleeves, sweetheart neckline, cinched waist, and wide flowing skirt were perfect for her body type. The deep discount, thanks to the color, held even more appeal.

Twirling in place, she smiled at the mirror. As a kid she'd always loved playing dress up in her mom's dresses. Tonight she felt a bit like Cinderella going to the ball with the prince. Or in this case, the baron.

Speaking—or thinking—of the devil, the doorbell sounded and grabbing her beaded clutch, she stopped herself from running and potentially tripping down the stairs and breaking her neck. Joan, on the other hand, in jeans had no issue bolting down the stairs and opening the front door.

Instead taking measured steps, she listened carefully to the introductions and pleasantries exchanged between Craig and Joan.

"She should be down any second. Would you like something to drink while you're waiting?"

"No, thank you. We really do have to leave. Traffic is more of a bear tonight than I expected."

No sooner were those last words out of his mouth when Kate turned on the landing taking the last three steps and caught site of Craig looking up. The way his jaw dropped slightly open before snapping shut and sporting a huge grin truly made her feel like Cinderella after her fairy godmother had done her work.

"You look stunning." He kept his eyes on her face. Such a gentleman. No wandering eyes, just a gleam of appreciation that made her feel a few inches taller.

"Thank you."

"Do you need a wrap?"

She shrugged. "I was going to pass on it in this heat, but then again, who knows how high the a/c will be cranked up."

"Is it upstairs?" Joan asked.

Kate nodded. "Still on the hanger in my closet."

A few seconds later, Joan was once again bolting down the stairs two at a time and gleefully handed over the matching wrap.

"Thanks."

"I want a full report when you come home!"

"Deal."

Like a true gentleman, Craig extended his arm and she slid her hand into the crook of his elbow.

"Don't get drunk and forget where you live!" Joan called out teasingly before closing the front door behind them.

"She was kidding." Kate looked up at him. "I don't have a drinking problem or anything."

"I didn't think you did," he reassured.

Still feeling very much the princess, her eyes almost fell out of their sockets when she spotted the car parked in her driveway. "Is that a Rolls Royce?"

"It is. Belongs to my father. The Mercedes is at the mechanics and I didn't think you wanted to climb into my Jeep or a ranch pickup."

"Thank you. Not in these heels." She really wanted to pinch herself. This was definitely a night that dreams were made of. Whether she was able to pitch her interests to the political bigwigs didn't seem to matter anymore. For tonight, she was simply going to enjoy living like the other half.

Most of his adult life, when Craig came through a door and attention turned in his direction, he knew it was the Baron name and reputation that attracted people. Tonight, he had no doubt at all it was the gorgeous woman on his arm. Even the women had to turn and look when they entered the ballroom.

When he glanced up from talking to Joan at the house and spotted Kate with one hand on the railing, slowly descending the last few steps, he thought he might swallow his tongue. Her hair was up but not in that large cartoon Texas way. Gentle locks of hair framed her face while swooping curls gathered in the perfect collection above her neck. And why was it he had an overwhelming need to nibble on the soft alabaster skin?

If he was going to make it through the night, he was going to have to stop focusing on Kate and keep his mind on the tedious political conversation that would no doubt ensue. Though it was clear to him from the way her gaze surveyed the room, she was not just eye candy for the night. Kate was a formidable woman.

Her hand still nestled in the crook of his arm, he leaned into and lowered his voice. "Who are we gunning for this evening?"

"Excuse me?"

The wide-eyed look on her face brought a grin to his

lips. "Who do you want to talk to about that project of yours?"

"Oh." She smiled back it him. "Congressman Korsak and Senator Pierce."

He knew both of those state representatives and for the first time, he actually felt sorry for them. "We're in luck." He pointed to the far corner of the room. "Shirley and Korsak are huddled with a few more of their colleagues by the back bar."

Her eyes narrowed and then a smile erupted when she had her targets in sight.

"I may suggest waiting a few more minutes. Korsak doesn't hold his liquor well. Give him a bit for his defenses to be down, but not so long that he doesn't remember what he agreed to."

Frown lines appeared on her forehead as she considered his words, then she nodded. "Makes sense. What about Senator Shirley Pierce?"

"She'll nurse that same glass of wine all night. I'm afraid you're on your own with her."

"I can handle that. I just needed to talk to them."

"May I suggest we take a turn on the dance floor while we wait for Korsak to relax?"

Her tentative smile brightened. "I would love that."

"Though I will warn you," he took her hand in his as they crossed the ballroom, "I'm mostly just a two step kind of guy."

"Funny. I'm mostly a two step kind of gal."

As if confirming their declarations, the DJ played a recognized country ballad and immediately the entire dance floor fell into the rhythm of circling the floor two steps at a time. A few of the couples clearly had danced together for years. The casual way they twirled out and then in without missing a beat. The smile on their faces. But mostly, the ability to move about as one. He'd always found it fascinating. As a matter of fact, if his grandparents were here, they would be one of those couples. As would his sister Eve and Jared. When those two stepped onto the dance floor, within minutes, everyone else moved away.

They'd made it around the floor several times when the song shifted to something more upbeat. Rather than continue and potentially reveal he actually had two left feet for anything besides two stepping, Craig gently steered Kate away from the floor. "I think there's been enough time passed."

Kate glanced in the direction Craig led them, her smile widening when she realized they were on a direct path to the two politicians she'd wanted to meet.

"Kate," a soft voice sounded beside them.

From the even broader smile that took over Kate's face, the petite brunette was clearly someone she liked. "Dr. Carter. What a nice surprise."

"Really? After all this time? It's Peg."

"Peg, do you know Craig Baron?" Kate waved a hand from the vet to him.

The doctor extended her hand. "Nice to meet you."

"Pleasure."

Peg turned back to Kate. "Head honcho at county animal services had to back out. Not sure how far down the list of people who could make nice with all these rich people they had to go through before they came upon little old me." She blinked and flashed a fast toothy grin at Craig. "No offense."

Her polite non-apology told him that the county animal services had picked the right gal to represent them. "None taken."

"Frankly, unlike Cinderella and her forest of friends, I don't get much chance to dress up. Could hardly wait, then I almost didn't make it. A few hours ago we were suddenly up to our eyeballs dealing with a sick—and uncooperative—raccoon."

"Rabbies?" It was the first thing that popped into Craig's mind.

The veterinarian shook her head. "No. An abscess that has been nothing but trouble and needed immediate surgery. Cyril is almost more pet than wild. He has had a chronic cheek infection since he could fit in my hand. He couldn't fend for himself in the wild so he has basically become a permanent resident of our facility."

"Peg is always going above and beyond when it comes to rehabbing and caring for our furry friends."

"Let's not exaggerate." Peg smiled.

Kate's brows rose on her forehead. "How many other animal rehab facilities were willing to keep Cyril?"

Peg shrugged. "Someone would have stepped up."

"Right." Kate dipped her chin in a single unconvinced motion.

"I need to go freshen up before I have to tackle our illustrious representatives and convince them our animals need these protections bills."

"I'll warm them up for you." Kate grinned.

"Oh, I like that." Peg's eyes twinkled. "A double whammy. Go get 'em. I'll be around shortly to seal the deal."

The two gave a discreet high-five and Kate slid her hand into Craig's elbow as they crossed the room. He could certainly get used to the feel of her so near.

"Craig. How nice to see you." Representative Korsak extended his hand and very casually glanced over Craig's shoulder, no doubt in search of his grandparents.

"Always a pleasure." Craig accepted the handshake and shifted, waving an arm at Kate. "Have you met Kate Donovan?"

"Can't say that I've had the pleasure." The older man extended his hand and any fool could see he was as smitten with Kate as most of the men in the room.

"Soliciting votes one by one, Stanley?" that came from Senator Shirley Pierce who turned to face Kate. "Don't let this geezer fool you. All he wants is your vote."

To her credit, Kate kept up her end of the polite chit-chat. The way she bade her time, participated in the benign political repartee, and waited to bring up the reason she'd been so eager to accompany Craig, told him this woman would have made a great negotiator. She was probably missing her call as a business mogul. At least the endangered animals in this world had a formidable advocate.

Right about the time words like waterways, industrial pollutants, and toxic chemicals were tossed around, the Austin diva came up behind him. "Craig. What a pleasant surprise." Without a second's hesitation for polite considerations, the woman slipped her hand into the crook of his arm and steered him away.

Looking over his shoulder, he reached out to touch Kate's arm and mouthed, "I'll be right back."

She nodded at him and totally focused, dove back into the conversation.

"So," the diva practically purred, "is she someone special?"

Craig had to stop and consider how to answer that one. After all, wanting to win the Academy Award-winning actress over to his production company, and hopefully new studio, didn't mean he had to wear his personal heart on his sleeve. "Isn't everyone in some way?"

The actress rolled her eyes. "You'd make a good politician yourself. Thinking of tossing your hat in the ring?"

That made him laugh. "Not even close. I have grease paint in my veins."

"I know what you mean. Once this business is in your blood, there's no escape." Slowing her steps, she waved at a few people huddled together. "You know Jim Stephens?"

Of course he did, and she knew it. The man's production company was responsible for some of the top rated shows on TV. Rumor had it he was looking to expand into film, and Craig didn't need to be hit over the head with a hammer to figure out the guy wanted to produce the same film Craig did. "Of course. Nice to see you again."

The next several minutes consisted of the most mundane chit-chat behind plastic Hollywood smiles. Neither dared mention the upcoming project that the diva held an option on, but it was obvious to any idiot that they both wanted a piece of the action. What Craig knew that no one else did was that he was about to put something on the table that dear Jim couldn't compete with. Pretty much everyone in Hollywood knew that she didn't take on many projects anymore because she didn't like the idea of leaving her family behind for months of filming. He knew for a fact that his new studio location was a mere two hours away from the actress' Texas home. If he could get it up and running sooner than later.

Still schmoozing the award-winning actress, and keeping an occasional eye on Kate deep in conversation across the hall, he could have been knocked over with a feather when Kate unexpectedly sidled up beside him. From the sweet smile and twinkling eyes, he'd venture a guess that her little chat had gone well.

To his surprise, when it came time to be seated for dinner, so engrossed in conversation with Kate over saving some bird—at least he thought a warbler was a bird—the famed actress had opted to sit at their table instead of her assigned place. Apparently, his ace in the hole for this deal might not be his stellar reputation or even the new Texas studio, but one Kate Donovan. And wasn't that just icing on the cake?

Never in her life had Kate felt more like Cinderella than tonight. She'd spent so much time smiling, her cheeks actually hurt more than her feet.

The valet pulled the Rolls sedan up in front of the downtown hotel. Handing the man what was most likely a hefty tip, Craig helped her into the car and then circled around to the driver's side.

Once they'd pulled away from the curb, he blended in with traffic and then turned to her. "Now that we're alone, what happened with the Senator and Korsak?"

Her hands clasped together in her lap, she felt like kicking her heels up. "There's legislation in the works to deal with the water pollution on Texas shores and its effect on wildlife. Well, not just the beaches. Our rivers have some major companies dumping a lot of toxins into the Texas waterways."

"That much I was able to follow."

"What I can't believe I didn't realize until now is that our elected officials don't actually pen much of our legislation."

"You mean the lobbyists."

She sprang around onto her hip to face him. "Yes!" Tugging at the seatbelt strap, she leaned back against the door. "I forgot you have a brother who's a senator."

"You may be the only one." He smiled, then lifted his hand waving off his last words. "Sorry. Go on."

"Well, I've been invited to Austin."

"Really?" He took his gaze off the road and looked at her with pride in his eyes. At least she thought that's what it might be.

Nodding, she smothered the urge to shriek with delight. "I'm going to be educating the task force on the problems we as environmentalists are seeing and how to better implement changes through legislation that will actually work. Hopefully now they'll put something out there that both sides of the fence can get behind."

"That sounds like a tall order."

She blew out a slow sigh. "The real world is never perfect, and I may not get even a fraction of what I'd like, but if I can make the slightest difference in the mangled mess the legislatures usually put forth, I'll be happy."

"Well done. If you ever want a job in politics, I know a U.S. senator who would love someone smart and caring."

"I do care. These animals, and even some families who are affected by the poison in the water tables, don't have anyone else to speak up for them."

"Erin Brockovich."

"I'm not going to pretend to be like her, but right now, I'm very happy with the outcome from tonight." She didn't bother mentioning how much being on his arm had added to the perfection of the evening.

"Listen," he reached out and put his hand on hers, "do you have plans for tomorrow? Around dusk?"

She shook her head. "I can finish up early if I have to. What do you have in mind?"

"It's a surprise, but I think you'll enjoy it. There's something on the ranch I want to show you."

"More baby cows?" She couldn't help smiling even wider. Baby animals were so adorable.

"I'm afraid no more calves." He laughed softly. "I'll pick you up around four thirty. Will that work?"

Her smile still plastered across her face, she nodded. "Sounds perfect." As a matter of fact, pretty much everything with Craig seemed to be more than perfect. Except the owls and their habitat. Why couldn't real life be more like fairytales? Perfect and happily ever after.

CHAPTER TWELVE

"**W**hy do you look like the cat who swallowed the canary?" Governor James Baron gave the growing puppy faithfully at his side one last pat before pushing to his feet.

First thing after meeting with Ted and uncovering the new bat problem, Craig had done what any intelligent, successful businessman with a timing problem would do; call his influential grandfather. Coming to a halt at the entry to the large but cozy family parlor, Craig addressed said grandfather. "I heard from your friend."

"Professor Stanwyck?"

"One and the same. I'm not even going to ask how you pulled this off, but there will be a team of grad students combing the new property, with Fish and Game approval, in the morning."

Sporting his stoic expression that revealed nothing, his grandfather cut the distance between them. "Field work is imperative to grad students. It was the perfect fit, a win-win for both sides."

"Now I'm crossing my fingers and toes that they don't uncover even more endangered species."

"From what Bob tells me, it's not that unusual to find an outlier in the animal kingdom who doesn't do what he's supposed to, but that they usually get with the program sooner than later."

"In other words, I shouldn't worry about over-hibernating striped watchamacallits?"

"Yeah. That about covers it, but that's an awfully happy look on your face over a bunch of grad students."

When Craig and his contemporaries were growing up,

that old man had eagle eyes, and obviously nothing had changed. "I'm having a picnic dinner with Kate tonight."

"Picnic?" His grandfather waggled his salt and pepper eyebrows.

"Thought she might enjoy the well diggers cave."

The Governor bobbed his head. "I bet she will. Especially if Hazel is packing your dinner."

"Fried chicken, cole slaw, home fried chips, and of course, fudge brownies. She tried to give us cake, but I figured the brownies would be more user-friendly."

"What time are you picking up your friend?" The Governor glanced at his watch. "You've got a short window till dusk."

"Actually, we decided it was silly for me to drive down to the burbs, come back here, then take her home, then drive back to the ranch again."

His grandfather didn't hold back a frown.

"I know." Craig raised his hand. "But she insisted."

The former Marine blew out a resigned sigh. "I'll never understand modern women."

Craig had to chuckle. He wasn't all that sure there was a man on the planet who fully understood any woman, ancient, old-fashioned, modern, or futuristic.

"And I believe that's your young lady." The Governor pointed to the car pulling up in the front drive.

His young lady. Boy, did he like the sound of that.

"Don't just stand there. Open the door for her," his grandfather groused at him, banging the cane he didn't really need on the floor. Some days the old man was more Marine than politician or family man. Tonight he was in full Marine mode.

Before Kate reached the top step, Craig held the front door open for her at the same time Hazel came running from the kitchen with a massive wicker basket in her arms. "I thought you might like a nice white wine to go with dinner."

Accepting the basket from the older woman who had cared for the Barons for as long as he could remember, Craig leaned over and kissed her cheek. "Perfect. Thank you, Hazel."

Like a schoolgirl, the woman giggled and blushed before turning on her heel and hurrying back to the kitchen.

Still standing in the doorway, Kate's gaze dropped to the container now in Craig's hands. "Nice basket."

Craig nodded. "What's inside is even nicer."

Her nose to the air, Kate sniffed. "Is that," a smile teased at the corners of her mouth, "brownies?"

"Maybe." He shrugged, then letting out a low chuckle, he nodded. "Sorry. Yes. And I will let you know that Hazel makes the best brownies in the county."

"That's an awful big basket for brownies."

"That's because there's more in here than just brownies." Craig tapped the wicker. "But you'll have to wait till we get where we're going to find out."

"Tease." She raised her brows and flashed a grin that could have melted the ice caps in the North Pole.

"You two had better get moving or it will be dark before you know it." The Governor leaned over and lifted up the dog that had followed him out of the parlor and was now tapping at his pant leg. "You know, you're going to be too big for this soon."

"That's because you spoil them." Grams came down the stairs, her gaze taking in the happenings in the foyer. "It's lovely to see you again, Kate."

"Thank you. It's nice to see you again, too."

"I hate to greet and run, Grams, but we'll be late if we don't get going."

A few more words exchanged and they were out the door, piled into his Jeep, and on their way down the side road that led to the portion of Baron land he wanted to share with his new friend.

"Is this the part where you finally tell me where we're going?" Kate tugged at her seatbelt.

"You already know from Hazel's basket that we're having a picnic dinner."

She shrugged. "Well, I figured out that we're having brownies for dessert. Does that count?"

"It does." He couldn't stop himself from smiling. Just

having her beside him was the better part of his day, but knowing that what he planned to share would probably bring that huge heartwarming smile to her face, only made him want to grin even wider. How he hoped he hadn't made the wrong choice for tonight.

"At least I have dessert figured out." Kate's day had been slammed. There wasn't a blessed thing she could do about the owl's nest except for Craig's sake, hope the eggs hatched sooner than later. But she'd hoped to at least help speed up the situation with the hibernating bats. Despite having been on the phone with just about every contact she had in every environmental agency and government office even slightly related to the situation, she still came up empty-handed. She'd so wished to have good news for him tonight. There was no point in bringing up an unsuccessful effort to speed along the process of securing the property for the new studio. Oddly, as annoyed as she'd been with Craig for even considering the property after discovering the owl, right now, she really wanted to see everything work out for both him and the birds. Having spent her entire day talking to everyone and anyone she thought might be able to help, she'd also skipped lunch, which right about now left her starving. "Curiosity is killing me. How much farther?"

"Almost there. A perk to Paradise Ridge being one of the bigger ranches in this part of Texas is that we have a lot of land, including some interesting landscape. The downside, of course, is some take longer to reach than others."

"The ranch is called Paradise Ridge?"

He nodded.

"I wondered what the PR stood for on the entry columns. Couldn't figure out where Baron fit it."

"It doesn't. The land belonged to my grandmother's family. They'd traveled all the way from Ireland. Settled first in Tennessee, and then when an opportunity to keep pushing west came, the Conroe's made it as far as Texas. Another day I'll take you to the ridge that the original homestead was on."

"Ooh, is there anything left of it?"

Smiling, he nodded again. "Just a single room log cabin, but it's still there. My grandmother makes sure of it. Anyhow, when all those settlers reached the ridge, my many times great-grandmother declared they'd reached paradise. They christened the original cabin on the hill Paradise Ridge. The name stayed with the ranch as they outgrew the cabin and acquired more land. It's always seemed fitting."

"I like it." She settled back in her seat and took in the pastures and scattering of cattle around them. The land wasn't the only thing about Paradise Ridge Ranch that she liked.

"Here we are." Craig drew the Jeep to a stop at the crest of a sloping hillside. "If you'll grab the blanket from the backseat, I'll bring the basket."

"Done." She reached over and grabbed the only blanket available, a soft but heavy patchwork quilt. The weight of it surprised her. It also told her that this sucker wasn't a store-bought polyester filled coverlet, but more likely a cotton filled quilt that had probably been in the family for generations. Helping Craig spread it out on the ground, she casually examined the stitching. As she'd suspected, it was hand sewn. "I hate to put this lovely piece on the grass."

The basket open and a bottle of wine in one hand and a large container in the other, Craig glanced down at the blanket. "We have a ton of those. I think every relative on all sides of the family that ever was, spent their entire lives sewing blankets to pass down for generations."

"Still." She fingered the colorful patterns.

"I'm not kidding. Grams has closets and blanket boxes overflowing with family quilts."

All set to argue that the old quilts were still something to be treasured, she was quickly distracted by the whiff of fried chicken that came her way. Having taken off the lid, the still warm chicken smelled absolutely heavenly.

"These are great too." Craig held out an open container

of orange chips. "Hazel is a whiz at homemade potato chips. Looks like she opted for sweet potato chips tonight."

"Oh my." Kate took one bite and decided homemade was a bazillion times better than store-bought.

"She adds cinnamon and some other secret ingredient she refuses to share with anyone."

"If she could package and sell these, she'd make a killing."

"Like all processed foods, I'm sure once someone tries to mass-produce it, they'll lose that special quality." He opened the lid on another container and waving a fork at her, extended his arm. "Cole slaw?"

Her mouth full of her first bite of chicken, she swallowed quickly. "Thank you."

"Also homemade. I wish Hazel made it more often."

Reaching for the proffered food, her hand lightly brushed against his. A spark of electricity shot up her arm and down her spine robbing her of her next breath. Just like an old-time movie, she'd have sworn she heard a string of violins playing. It took every ounce of will power she had not to lean forward, pull him close and see what the rest of the orchestra would sound like.

The way Craig's eyes darkened and his jaw tightened, she was pretty sure she wasn't the only one who felt the unexpected connection. The question, of course, was what the heck was she going to do about it?

Not that she had a chance to even think it through. Clearing his throat, Craig pulled away and replaced the lid on the container. "I think you'll like it. The cole slaw."

Reason and good sense pushing spontaneity and playing with fire aside, all she could do was nod and take a bite. "Oh, my." She waved her fork at the plate. "I honestly think this is the best cole slaw I've ever had in my life."

"Don't doubt it." Setting his overflowing paper plate on the blanket, Craig let out a long sigh, whether it was at the lost opportunity, or something else, she had no idea. "The sun will be setting soon." He pointed down the hillside. "I want you to keep your eyes on that crop of mesquites down by the foot of the next hill."

A fried chicken wing in hand, she squinted down to the trees he gestured toward. "What's down there?"

"Not much." Something in the way the twinkle in his eyes matched his lazy smile warned her there was definitely something going on down there.

So intent on understanding what was so important about a clump of trees at the bottom of a hill, she forgot all about the food.

"More chicken?" Craig held the container out again.

She shook her head. "No, thank you." Her initial hunger appeased, she was now much more intrigued by the trees and what Craig had up his sleeve.

"If it helps any, I will tell you those trees are actually hiding the mouth of an old cave."

"A cave? In the middle of a pasture?"

Craig shrugged. "Who am I to argue with Mother Nature?"

Nibbling on another piece of chicken, she wished Craig would just tell her what was happening.

"It's about the right time." He pulled out his phone and smiled at her. "Pay attention."

"I am." She didn't dare drag her gaze away from the bottom of the hill. Though she did think he was nuts because any minute now, they'd be sitting at the top of a hill in the pitch black of night, eating food they wouldn't be able to see. And then it happened. She heard a rustling sound and once she blinked, a rush of dark swooped up from the trees.

Within seconds the once darkening blue skies was almost covered in a wave of black specks flying up and over. The movement of wings and air created a rushing sound overhead. It took her another second to process the magnificent sight of black ribbons swirling like snakes against a now red, pink, and graying sky. *Bats*!

"Wow." She dared steal a glance in his direction. If it was possible, his satisfied smile outdid the Cheshire Cat.

"Thought you'd like that."

The rushing sound continued overhead as what felt like millions of bats flew around overhead before flying out of sight in search of food. Her hand over her mouth, she couldn't find words for the amazing performance.

"As kids in the summer we used to lie here for hours waiting for night-time when they'd swoosh out of their caves. Of course, come fall they migrate south to warmer weather, but we all feel pretty privileged to have them here."

"I've told myself for years that the next time I'm in Austin I was going to play tourist and watch the bats fly. This is so much better." Without thinking, she twisted around and flung her arms around him. "Thank you!"

CHAPTER THIRTEEN

The feel of Kate enthusiastically pressed against him was a temptation too great to resist. Without thought, his arms settled around her waist and held her in place. As their gazes locked, the setting sun nearly gone, all he could see was the surprise in her eyes. He couldn't for the life of him determine if that wide-eyed look was one of anticipation or distress. As far as he was concerned, there was only one way to find out.

Lowering his head, he hesitated only inches away from her face. Doing his best to read the bevy of emotions and thoughts behind her steady gaze, not seeing any signs of apprehension, he closed the gap between them. Letting their mouths meld in a gentle and tender kiss that tasted even sweeter than he'd expected. That same sweetness told him to back up before he got himself into trouble.

When he leaned back, but kept his hands loosely around Kate's middle, he waited for a sign of whether or not he'd totally screwed things up. It took longer than he liked, but the tip of her tongue peeked out, moistening her lips, and then, to his utter delight, a sweet, slow smile stretched across her face.

"That was nice."

His cheeks tugged eagerly at the corners of his lips. "Better than nice."

Now he saw the blush creep across her cheeks and couldn't think of anything more beautiful than Kate in the burgeoning moonlight. Closing his eyes a moment, he debated whether or not he dared to inch in for another kiss, or do the smarter thing and back up while he still had the good sense to do so. Everything in him screamed don't let her go, except for the still small voice in the back of his head warning him only fools rush in.

Forcing his arms to relinquish their hold on her, he leaned fully away, carefully putting more distance between them. "Shall we finish dinner in the moonlight, or would you prefer to head back to the house and eat on real furniture?"

Her chin dipped as she seemed to study the quilt underneath them. "It's a lovely night."

That it was.

"The moonlight is pretty bright."

This time he nodded and resisted the urge to kiss the exposed skin on her neck as she glanced up at the sky.

"Look at all those stars."

It took everything in him to tear his gaze away from her and turn to the skies he knew so well.

"It's hard to believe how close we are to Houston and yet I've never seen stars like this at my house."

"No competing lights. Makes you understand why writers are always comparing the night sky to black velvet."

"Diamonds on black velvet."

He bobbed his head and blowing out a restless sigh, reached for the fried chicken and held it out to Kate. "More food?"

"No, thank you. Though..." Grinning again, she reached across him and retrieved a few chips. "We really do need to find out what it is that Hazel puts on these besides cinnamon."

And just like that, everything was back to normal. "I have an update on the other bat situation."

To his surprise, Kate pressed her lips together tightly, closed her eyes and shook her head. "They told you?"

"Who told me what?"

She shrugged. "Any one of the nine million people I called today. I'm sorry. I tried. I really did. And I didn't want anyone to bother you with it. Did someone complain about how pushy I was?" Her eyes widened and her jaw dropped. "Oh, no. Did one of the agencies complain to your brother? I didn't want to get anyone in any trouble. I just wanted to help."

None of what she'd just said made any sense until his mind wrapped itself around her last words – she just wanted to help. Help how? "Would I totally ruin the evening if I admitted I have no idea what you're talking about?"

"You don't?" The look of abject panic was replaced with a good dose of confusion.

He shook his head. "Sorry, no."

"Maybe you should just tell me what your updates are."

If he'd learned anything from having three younger sisters, it was that the safest strategy a man could take—in any situation—was to follow the woman's lead. "A team of grad students will be scouring the property for hibernating bats starting tomorrow."

"They will?" Her eyes opened wide again and her voice rose an octave in surprise. "Really?"

"Yeah. I felt the same way when I got the call from Professor Stanwyck."

A deep-set frown settled over narrowed eyes. "That's so odd. When I called around today, if I heard 'Lady, that's not how it works' once, I heard it a hundred times. How did you get them to put a team together so fast?"

"Not me." He shrugged. "My grandfather."

"It's not what you know but who you know." Her head bobbed up and down. "Of course." He wished those last two words didn't sound so condemning.

"I'm sorry if pulling strings is upsetting to you, but his heart was in the right place." It always was.

Again, she shook her head. "For once I'm glad power and connections worked. I tried to do the same thing. I just don't have the clout of a former governor."

"But you're better looking if that helps." His brows rose high on his forehead and his smile pleaded with her to not be upset.

She really wasn't at all. Yes, there were plenty of times

when she would be furious at the privilege that came with money and power and a dirty fight, but in this case, she was just plain happy that someone had managed to speed things up for him. "So, what's the plan now?"

"Unfortunately, I have to fly out to tomorrow afternoon. Some complications on a set in LA. I had to sell my first born to get them to let us film on Malibu beach."

"You don't have children." Or had she missed something about him?

A deep chuckle erupted. "Sorry, that was just an expression. My mother says my occasional flair for overdramatic is what makes me a good producer."

"I haven't noticed you being overly dramatic."

"Thank you. I don't think I am, but there are problems on the set. I had to swear up and down that there would be no parking on the street. That meant we had to figure out how to configure gear, the grip truck—"

"Grip truck?"

"Sorry, a grip truck is a six ton vehicle like a big moving truck that transports all equipment other than cameras, like film, etc. Then we needed to work out where to put the makeup and hair trailer, the star trailer."

"All the things you need space for on the lot here in Texas."

A broad smile cut across his face. "You remembered. Yes. All those things and more. We need to keep it all behind a gate and we only have access to one little driveway. Of course it would have been much easier if the A-list star across the street—who happens to be out of town filming a movie in Paris—had not been such a twit and allowed us to park in his empty driveway."

"That doesn't seem very neighborly. Are all A-list stars that mean?"

"No, but the shuttle system we set up isn't working and someone needs to get out there and renegotiate how we're going to pull this filming off without totally blowing the budget or getting thrown out of town."

"Will you be back for Friday?"

"Come hell or high water." He snickered softly. "Even

if it means selling my second born."

That made Kate laugh. What was it about this man that so easily made her want to smile? "Maybe I should have tried that."

"Selling your second born?" Craig teased.

Kate nodded. "One of my many conversations today was with the new Fish and Game guy assigned to our case."

"Not as friendly as Ted?"

This time she shook her head and tugged at a piece of grass beside her. "I'm not sure if he's overwhelmed, under informed, or just difficult."

"Uh oh. That doesn't sound good."

Her spine stiffened and lifting her chin in the air like a royal princess whose corset is too tight, she mimicked the new guy. "I can't possibly process this overnight. There is a huge stack of cases ahead of yours. It wouldn't be fair to expedite your situation."

"Did he really sound like that?" Craig leaned back on his elbows.

"Worse. I don't know if he has a cold or shares genetics with Arnold Horshack."

"Who?"

She bit back a laugh and shaking her head, waved a hand at nothing in particular. "Sorry. Mom loves retro TV. Horshack is a character from an old TV show who talked through his nose."

"Ah. I see. Well, the important thing is the professor and his team are coming to get the ball rolling on clearing this situation up."

Leaning back beside him, her gaze drifted to the velvety sky. "Nights like this can make a person wish that tomorrow didn't have to come."

"The stars are beautiful."

"They really are." She didn't see any point in mentioning the stars were the smallest part about this evening that had her wishing it didn't have to end. The landscape was great, but it was the company that made all the difference. She wasn't sure how long they stayed on the quilt, staring at the stars, sharing few words. As odd as it was, she'd never felt so comfortable sitting silently with another person.

When Craig leaned forward and began gathering the remnants of dinner into the basket, she almost blew out a heavy sigh of disappointment. Of course the evening had to come to an end, and stomping her feet like a three-year-old to make it known she wasn't ready to leave, would not be the best idea she'd ever had. "What time does your flight leave?"

Standing up, the picnic basket looped on one arm, he extended his hand to her and gently tugged her onto her feet. "Not till two o'clock. Morning flights are all sold out. Besides, I want to meet the environmental team at the property. At least establish some hint of a working relationship."

That wasn't a half-bad idea at all. Not that his charming demeanor, or Baron name, would make a difference on the what the team found, but then again, what did she really know about the Baron influence. Clearly, it had moved mountains she couldn't even reach. "I'd like to come too, if that's okay."

Even with only moonlight she could see that lazy smile that made her insides do somersaults, start to tip upward on one side. "More than okay."

Returning the smile, she turned to gather up the blanket, carefully folding and tucking it under one arm. "Ready?"

Craig nodded. His smile turning more tentative, he extended his free hand in front of her. "Okay?"

Her heart did a quick Texas two step at the proffered hand. Easing hers into his, she reveled in the gentle strength of his fingers protectively closing around hers. "More than okay."

A big part of her no longer seemed to care about the bats, the owls, or the eggs in the nest. All her years of experience told her this entire scenario was unlikely to end well for Craig and his project, and that there wasn't a blessed thing she could do to change the outcome. But at this particular moment in time, she really hoped that team Baron could come up with a miracle.

CHAPTER FOURTEEN

For the first time since he was an anxious teen anticipating prom night, or more so, the after-parties, Craig could not stop thinking about Kate under the moonlight or how badly he had wanted to kiss her and never stop. Everything about last night had been perfect. Everything about Kate was perfect. More than perfect. Every smile made him more determined to be the one to keep that smile on her face. To hand her the world on a silver platter, even if that meant singlehandedly saving every animal on the planet.

He was being absolutely ridiculous. He knew it, and yet, there wasn't a thing he could do about it. If his brothers could see him now, they wouldn't let him hear the end of it. Who would ever have believed that making one woman happy would become more important than money, business, or even the art of the deal. This beautiful, caring woman had worked her way under his skin and into his mind and, blast, his heart too. So this morning's question was what the heck was he supposed to do about it?

Nervously tapping his college ring against the steering wheel, his mind darted from the logistics problem in LA, to the team holding his business plans in their hands, to the woman he reluctantly walked away from after a long drive and short kiss goodnight on the front porch. If the professor's report pitted him against Kate, how the heck was he going to handle it? Tapping his ring at a faster beat, he shook his head slowly. He never thought there would be a day he would find himself even considering tossing a huge chunk of money down a rat hole for the love of a woman. And there was that word again, dancing around his mind and heart. Was this really it? Like his brothers before him, had he found *the* one? The woman he could grow old with like his grandparents? Blowing out a heavy sigh, he pulled onto the dirt drive and was still as confused and anxious as he'd been when he'd tossed and turned most of the night.

Bouncing down the ruts and dips in the road, the number of cars parked to one side of the drive surprised him. Just how many grad students did the environmental team need? Pulling in to park in front of the long line of cars, his gut sank at the sight of the Fish and Game truck. Hadn't the new guy told both him and Kate he didn't have time for this project? What the heck was he doing here?

On the other side of the vehicle, he spotted Kate's car. He hadn't expected her to beat him here. Holding his hand over his brows, shading his eyes from the morning sun and not seeing Kate or anyone in sight, it suddenly occurred to him, what if the fish guy wasn't the new guy but Ted? What if he'd found time for the project, and for Kate? Those thoughts had him picking up his pace, marching to the other side of the barn where Ted had first mentioned finding the yellow striped whatchamacallit.

As he turned the corner, he almost tripped over his own tongue. An army of ants couldn't have outnumbered or outmaneuvered the number of people slowly moving about the open field. It took another moment of observation to process how carefully the crowd was moving. They really were like a well-formed army of something.

"They've been here since the crack of dawn." A tall gentleman in jeans and a college sweatshirt tapped at his phone, slipped it into his pocket and extended his hand. "I'm Bob Stanwyck."

"Nice to meet you." As casually as he could, Craig glanced over the man's shoulder for any sign of Kate.

"If you're looking for your friend, she and the agency guy are at the original nest site."

It took a few seconds to realize he meant the hibernating bats, not the owl. "I see."

"I stepped away to take a call. I suspect they're still

over there…discussing the situation."

Oh, he didn't like the sound of that. Falling into step beside the professor, he resisted the urge to push past the guy and find Kate quickly. It had taken another few minutes before he recognized the woman in the distance. Standing beside an area sectioned off with yellow tape that reminded Craig of a television crime scene, her hands on her hips, her elbows flaring like chicken wings, any fool could see Kate was not happy.

"That's absurd," she groused.

The man in uniform who Craig was delighted to see was not the smitten Ted, shook his head. "Ma'am, I'm only following rules."

"Guidelines are meant to be just that, guides. Not hard-and-fast rules without flexibility."

Still shaking his head, the man who looked to be younger than some of the grad students combing the property showed no sign of caring what she said, never mind actually listening.

Something deep in Craig's gut told him that he did not want to know what they were arguing about, and yet, here he was closing in on the two of them. "Did I miss something?"

Kate spun about, teeth clenched, and blowing out a sigh, closed the short distance between them. "So far the team has only found one active site. They've also found two abandoned nests. No bats."

"That's good." Craig nodded, wondering what was he missing. No man or woman alive got prickly over good news.

"It would be." Standing only inches away from him, she blew out another deep long breath. "Alan here wants to shut everything down." Her eyes narrowed in the guy's direction. "And I mean everything. No cars, no contractors, no owners, nothing."

Something wasn't computing. *Wait.* "Owners? As in me?"

Her head bobbed forcefully as she slapped the tip of her finger on her nose. "Give the man a prize. It might be time to have another chat with your grandfather. I'm heading back to my car to call Ted."

Tablet in hand, the government guy straightened his shoulders and stared daggers at Kate.

Craig wasn't so sure he liked that any better than Ted's starry eyes.

"If by his grandfather, you mean the former Governor Baron…"

Nothing in the man's tone said that he had a fondness for the family name. As a matter of fact, the word that came to mind was disdain.

Alan shook his head. "The *former* governor is not my boss."

Kate stopped in her tracks, looked to him, then Alan, and then back to him again. For a moment he thought for sure when he saw her mouth fall slightly open that fire would spew forth. Instead, she snapped her mouth shut, shook her head, and stormed back toward the barn until the squawking above had her stopping to look up.

Craig pulled out his phone. Tapping away, he ignored Alan and hurried after Kate. One thing he'd mastered in his time is of the essence career was the art of walking, talking, chewing gum, and texting at the same time.

Pausing to stare upward, Kate shook her head, then started walking again. "One of the owls seems a bit talkative this morning. Odd."

"A talking bird?" he chuckled. "Yeah. Odd's a good word."

Not bothering to look at him, she simply shook her head and continued toward the barn door.

Craig glanced over his shoulder, unexpectedly pleased that Alan had stayed where he was, barking at the grad students working. Looking back to Kate, he wondered why she kept looking up at the owl soaring over the barn. What was the big deal? When her pace picked up, a prickling sensation shot up his spine. He hadn't a clue what was up, but he quickened his step nonetheless.

As quickly as Kate had hurried into the barn, she was just as quickly rushing back.

"What's wrong?"

She hefted her hands onto her hip again, and spoke to him while staring up at the still soaring bird. "Usually mama owl sits on the nest for about twenty-three hours a day, but when she takes a break to get some food, papa owl comes and minds the roost."

"Okay."

She shook her head. "No one is minding the nest. Which means one of the parents is playing hooky, drunk, or both."

Now he was completely confused.

"Something's not right." Frowning, she moved in the same direction the bird kept circling. When the squawks seemed to increase in pitch and volume, both Kate and he slowed their steps. Both scanning the surroundings. No one had said a word, and yet, they both seemed to know what to do.

"There." Her arm shot out straight from the shoulder and she ran ahead with the speed of a medal winning sprinter. "Oh, no!"

The moment her heart had begun to thump in her chest like a hammer pounding a nail, Kate knew something was wrong. For days, her heart had been kicking up its heels whenever Craig was around, but this frantic pounding had less to do with animal attraction and everything to do with an overwhelming sense of dread. The mound of snowy white at her feet pulled a sudden screech from deep in her throat. The limp mama bird tore at Kate's heart strings. Dropping to her knees, she hovered over the bird.

"How bad is she hurt?" Craig came sliding onto the ground beside her. Without waiting for a response, he laid his hand on the bird's chest and turned to Kate. "It's breathing, but I've no idea if it's struggling to do so."

"We have to get her to treatment." Kate ripped off her sweatshirt, exposing her Go Green t-shirt. Gently, she covered the bird and swooped it into her arms.

"Here. Let me." Craig wrapped the claws in the remaining shirt and retrieved the fowl from Kate's arms. "If he or she comes to, I don't want it scratching the dickens out of you."

The thought of explaining, in clearly enunciated syllables, that she could handle a frantic owl with her eyes closed had crossed her mind, along with a flash of temper, but the look in Craig's eyes stopped her short. Was this the same man who said business was business and the owl could live on someone else's land? The care and tenderness the man showed for the sick bird smacked her on the chest and squeezed her heart.

"Where do we take her?" He was already hurrying toward the car.

"Peg's wildlife rescue center isn't far from here. I'll call ahead." She pulled out her phone and looked up to the owl's mate still screeching overhead. "I'll also see if we can pull some of the grad students to catch Papa and gather the eggs. We've got to keep them warm. Hopefully, Mama hadn't been gone long."

"Otherwise…" Craig looked toward the bird.

"Otherwise," Kate finished for him, "your owl problem could be gone."

His head moved from side to side. "I'd rather have the problem."

"What are you doing?" Alan's gaze settled on the clothing and bird in Craig's arms.

"Taking this sick owl to the bird doctor."

"Sick?" Alan moved closer and with one finger, pulled the sweatshirt away.

"We really need to go," Craig spoke to the man now moving the bird gently about.

Alan's jaw tightened and his eyes narrowed. "Damn. She's not sick. She's been shot. I'm going to have to call this in. A team of specialists will be sent, then we can move her to one of our clinics."

"Sent?" Craig stared at the guy as if his brains had just fallen out his ears.

"Yeah." Alan held the phone in his hand. "I can't move the bird, I have to stay on site with those students."

"We. Can't. Wait." Craig's voice fell a fraction short of yelling.

Alan lifted the phone to his ear. "We have no choice. Rules are rules."

One of the key things about environmentalism was that they tended to go hand in hand with the idea of a violence-free, peaceful life. Right now, Kate had little interest in peace, and the idea of violence against anyone who would hurt such a beautiful bird sounded better with every tick of the clock. Ignoring Alan, she waved one of the students over, told her what she needed, and then watched the eager young woman gather a larger crew, directing some toward the nest and others to track down the injured bird's mate. Thank heaven others were here to help. Kate had a feeling if she wandered away, there might be bloodshed. From the daggers the students were staring at Alan with, it appeared the number of people willing to slug the guy was growing exponentially.

"Rules, my foot." Rolling his eyes heavenward, Craig turned away from the by-the-book field officer and began marching toward the car in a quick clip, shouting over his shoulder to Kate, "I'm guessing if she's been shot she's not going to suddenly wake up. I'll drive if you'll take the bird."

She lengthened her stride to keep up with him, trusting the students to save the eggs. "I can drive."

Stopping by the passenger side of his vehicle, he shook his head and handed her the bird. "Trust me when I tell you, we'll get anywhere faster if I drive."

She had no idea if she should be thankful or run for the hills. Apparently, she was about to find out.

CHAPTER FIFTEEN

When Craig said that he could drive anywhere faster, the man wasn't kidding. Doing her best to cradle the bird carefully in one arm, with every wild turn she used the other to grip the dashboard and keep them from falling over into Craig's lap. Or worse, out the door altogether. There were fingernail gouges in the car to prove it.

Once they'd reached the small clinic, she was tempted to get down on all fours and kiss the concrete. Apparently, the need for speed was a genetic thing with the Barons. She hadn't dared look, but she was pretty sure the man was flying down those country roads at something in the ballpark of ninety or a hundred miles an hour. The only reason the words *slow down* didn't rip from her throat was that her fear of the bird dying before they could get help was greater than her fear of Craig wrapping the car around a tree.

As the car came to a screeching halt in front of the veterinarian's office, Peg and another woman Kate didn't recognize came running out to meet them halfway to the door. Other vets would have waited for her to come in with the injured bird. Not Peg. Just one reason she would always be one notch above the others in her field.

"We'll take it from here." The doc scooped the bird out of Kate's grip. "How long ago was she hit?"

"We don't know. I don't even know how it happened. The Fish and Game officer said she's been shot."

The doc nodded and once inside, hurried down the hall without asking any further questions.

Only because of her previous visits did Kate know that

the doc had rushed past the regular exam rooms and pushed through the door to the operating room.

"Who would do such a thing?" Kate paced in the small veterinary waiting room, desperately trying to expel all her nervous energy. Anyone would think it was her child and not a wild bird inside. "I wonder how long she'd been hurt?"

"I don't know the answers to either question." The way Craig's jaw clenched, anyone could see he was as concerned about the owl as she was. "But the important thing is we got mama bird to someone who can help."

Pacing, Kate had lost track of time. Questions ricocheted in her mind one after the other: who would do such a thing, had they found her in time, was it too late for Peg to help, did the grad students corral her mate, were the eggs on their way. With every unanswered thought, her heart hammered more forcefully in her chest. Taking in a long, deep breath, Kate stopped her pacing and glanced down the hall.

The weight of Craig's arm suddenly draped around her shoulder sent a ray of calm through her system. Tucked in at his side, he gently whispered against her temple, "It's going to be fine. You told me Peg's one of the best."

Leaning her head against him, she took a long moment to just breathe in his strength and confidence. "That's because she is."

Now his fingers tenderly drew soothing circles against her shoulder. "She has that look about her that reminds me of my Grams on a mission."

That made Kate chuckle. She didn't know Lila Baron well, but she would certainly trust the older woman with a sick anything. "Peg's been building this rehab sanctuary for years. Thankfully, the other night was the first time I've seen her in a while. I'm hoping right about now this is one of those no news is good news scenarios."

"Hopefully, someone will be out soon to tell us mama owl is on the road to recovery." He brushed a stray lock of hair behind her ear. "It'll be all right. You'll see. Peg has a nice face. She won't let you down."

An unexpected urge to chuckle tickled her throat. If only people's skills could really be determined by a nice face. "I wonder how those students are doing with the eggs?"

No sooner were the words out of her mouth than the front door blew open and two young women carrying a small blanket-covered box tore into the room. "We've brought the eggs. Tim rigged something with a flashlight under the blanket for warmth but they need a real incubator."

Though she'd have rather stayed encircled in the comforting warmth of Craig's arms like a blanket on a winter's day, Kate pulled away and approached the two women. Before she could say a word, the woman behind the reception desk jumped to her feet. "This way."

With a simple curling of her finger, everyone followed the receptionist down the hall.

"The doc is pretty short-handed. Every time the economy hits a rough spot our donations drop and we find ourselves managing on a shoestring budget." The woman fiddled with the incubator that reminded Kate of an old ice cream maker before carefully placing each egg in the contraption. "But these back-to-back years have taken a harder hit. The doc, me and the tech inside with her now are all the staff we can afford, and we all took pay cuts to keep this place running. We have to send all the rehabs to Dallas. Some to Austin."

"Peg never said a word to me." Kate couldn't believe such a wonderful program was struggling and that she'd had no idea. All their chit-chat the other night about pro-environmental legislation and the good doctor had not given even a small hint of her own problems.

"Hey." Craig reached over and gently ran the back of his hand down her arm. "You okay?"

She shook her head. "We need Peg. She's good. She cares. Not that all veterinarians don't care, but she always goes the extra mile. Does so much for our injured." Kate bit down on her lower lip. She didn't want to lose this beautiful bird, and Texas wildlife couldn't afford to lose Peg's rehab program. What in the name of all that was holy had gone wrong with this world?

Never in his entire life had Craig wanted anything more than to keep Kate in his arms, deliver a healthy and happy owl to her, and make sure that she never had to worry about anything else in her life. The problem, of course, was that all the power, influence, and money in the world couldn't guarantee any of the above. Not even his expert fixer of a grandfather could save the bird if the vet could not, or ensure Kate's happiness.

The double doors at the end of the hall sprang open, and rolling her neck, Peg strolled toward him. Her expression carried fatigue, but nothing else he could read. When she came within a few feet of them, the veterinarian formed a wide grin. "No promises yet, but I'm very optimistic."

He'd been unprepared for Kate to spin about and throw her arms around him. Squeezing him tightly, she inched back, and grinning up at him, squealed, "We got to her in time."

"Barely," Peg interjected before he could forget where they were and kiss those delectable lips, audience be damned.

Inching away from him, Kate stepped toward the veterinarian. "Was she really shot?"

Peg bobbed her head. "With a BB gun. Probably kids."

"That's what we think." The voice behind them came from an officer who had quietly entered the clinic. "I just heard from another officer on the scene."

Kate's brows buckled with confusion, but Craig was the one to ask, "Who called the police?"

Clearing his throat, the officer sighed. "I have no idea, but whoever it was, they had my sergeant rushing us to investigate. I'm here to see what the doc can tell us; the other officers are on the scene of the crime."

There was no need to ask for further information.

Craig's quick text to his grandfather to apprise him of Agent Rules-Are-Rules as potential trouble had led to his grandfather calling while they were on the way to the clinic. There had been no time to go into details, but the abridged version had been enough. Clearly, the Governor had not lost his touch.

"According to the update I received, they've stumbled across what we believe are the remnants of hollow logs destroyed by explosives."

"Explosives?" Kate backed up against Craig's chest and he immediately sensed the tension returning to her body.

"Yes, ma'am. It's not unusual to find bored kids in the country blowing up hollow logs."

"Or shooting BB guns," Craig interjected.

"Exactly." The tall uniformed man nodded.

"I didn't know the police got involved in bird shootings," one of the two students who'd brought in the eggs commented.

"I admit, normally we wouldn't have gotten on this so quickly, but it's always a risk that shooting at animals is the springboard to more dangerous issues." Rubbing at the back of his jaw with one finger, the man sprouted a lazy smile. "Having Governor Baron be the one to alert us didn't hurt any. Though in this part of the county, we're more likely to be called out because some teens went toilet paper happy redecorating someone's front yard or tipping cows."

"Wait a minute." Kate held up her hand. "Where do kids get explosives?"

The officer half raised a noncommittal shoulder. "Borrowed from Mom and Dad's ranch stash, stolen from a construction site; too many possibilities, certainly more than any of us like."

"So now what?" Kate asked.

The officer turned to Peg. "Don't suppose you have any information that might confirm it was just kids being stupid."

"Afraid not." Arms crossed, the vet shook her head. "BBs aren't like bullets that can be traced with ballistics, but I do hope somehow you figure it out. I don't need some stupid kids taking pot shots at more wild birds. Or worse."

"Amen," Kate agreed. "How soon before she can return to her nest and family?"

Her lips pressed tightly together, the doc shook her head ever so slightly. "Depends. I don't have the staff anymore to do the care she'll need. I'm going to watch her myself overnight. If all goes well, tomorrow we'll find a volunteer to transport her to Dallas. We've checked and they have room to rehab a large bird. They'll want the mate too. He's probably frantic."

"And the eggs?" Craig was just as worried about the baby owls.

The doc looked to her tech who had disappeared with the incubator and just recently returned.

"All eggs still viable." The tech smiled.

"Good." The doc turned back to Kate. "We'll send mama bird and the eggs to the rehab facility. I'm sorry I can't do more."

"I can't thank you enough for what you've done so far." Kate inched forward and gave Peg a quick hug. "We'll take care of finding her mate."

The only one to remain behind talking with the vet was the police officer. Kate looked down at her phone and scanned the incoming texts. "Seems Alan is getting testy."

That was no surprise to Craig. He'd almost prefer Ted had returned to the site. Hopefully, whoever else his grandfather had called would be able to step in and keep Alan in line.

"You know what this means?" Kate stood by the passenger door of Craig's car.

Standing close enough to Kate to smell the lingering scent of vanilla shampoo in her hair, his mind was racing in all different directions. There wasn't a chance in hell he could currently add two and two, never mind answer her question. "What?"

"With the owls moved, you've lost a major obstacle to your construction plans."

"Oh, that."

Her eyes widened and her brows lifted high on her

forehead a fraction of a second before she chuckled softly. "They get under your skin, don't they."

"They?"

"Defenseless animals."

"Owls aren't all that defenseless, and frankly, I'm not sure about those bats, but yeah, I have a much better handle on why you love what you do." Not caring who might be lingering on the sidewalk, he looped his arms around her waist and pulled her in close. "There are a lot of things I love about you, Katherine Donovan, and how much you care for the animal kingdom is only one of them."

"Love?" Her voice cracked ever so slightly.

Leveling his gaze with hers, he searched for any sign of what was running through her mind. Without a clue, he opted to jump in with both feet. He'd never been afraid of taking risks and now was no time to start. "I love you, Kate."

Again, her eyes rounded before a bright smile brought a sparkle to her gaze. "And I love you back."

Swallowing the urge to shout *Yeehaw* and spin her around, instead, he did what he'd wanted to do all day. He lowered his head until his lips touched hers. Ever so sweet, he pulled her closer and did his best to show her just how much she meant to him.

CHAPTER SIXTEEN

What had started out as a miserable day, dealing with Fish and Game's finest, the grad students, finding the female owl, the vet's office, the bats, and finally catching and transporting the owl's mate, should have left her exhausted and drained. Instead, Craig's declaration of love and the kiss that still had her toes tingling, had left her flying high as the birds she so loved and ready to take on the world, and win. Blinking a couple of times, she glanced over at Craig, delighted that he'd kept his hold on her hand the entire ride.

"I've been doing a little thinking."

"Careful you don't hurt yourself." She did her best to suppress a grin at her tease.

"Ha, ha, ha." His smile widened and his hold on her hand tightened just enough to reassure he got the joke.

"What about?" she asked.

"Peg's situation."

"Oh." In between rushing back and forth and dealing with everyone on the property about the birds and the bats and Alan's attitude, she'd tried to come up with some way to help Peg and the rehab program she'd run for so long. "I still can't believe I hadn't heard what a hard time she's having."

"As small as the world gets at times, it's still a very big place."

"So what are you thinking?"

"I had a few minutes while you were going over the report with the police to look Peg up on my phone. She's more than qualified and has even had a few articles written on the good work she's done. I think with the right backing, her facility could outshine the ones in Dallas or Austin."

"In some ways, she already does."

He bobbed his head and pressed his lips together a long moment, making Kate wonder what was he trying to tell her.

"The Barons sit on an awful lot of boards of different foundations. We volunteer everywhere, and write checks like we're pouring another glass of water. Not long ago my grandparents got on board a new charity project with my sister Eve's fiancé."

"For children of veterans. I love that idea."

Craig smiled. "We all do. Grams especially loves a worthwhile project. I'm thinking, perhaps the right someone," he held her hand up slightly and smiled at her, "could persuade Grams to take on another worthy cause. The Barons aren't the only ones who write checks."

"Really?" Tugging at the seatbelt, she swung around to face him. If he weren't driving, she'd have thrown herself over the console for a stuffing squishing hug. "That would be great."

"Peg's practice is important to the neighboring communities. The Houston area is massive. The more people encroach natural habitats, the more we need facilities like Peg's."

"Agreed."

"Good, because I cut her a small check to hire some more help until we can get some serious fundraising going for her."

This time she didn't care. Unlatching her seatbelt, she pushed up, leaned over the console, and kissed him gently on the cheek before sitting back and buckling up again. "I love you, Craig Baron."

His cheeks actually tinged pink as his smile widened. "Then maybe I should wait till we get you home to tell you the rest of my thoughts when you can thank me properly."

For that, she smacked his arm lightly with her free hand. "Comedian. What else have you got up your sleeve?"

"My studio is going to be one of those properties encroaching on natural habitats."

She nodded. That was only one of the reasons she was originally against the idea of his using the land for a movie studio.

"I've asked Devlin to look into buying more surrounding land. This will make it easier to create a buffer zone around the studio. Keep the area a safe habitat for owls and other creatures. Plant more trees. Build owl houses. Plant more low-growing grasses or whatever rodents and other members of the food chain like to live in."

"I hate to keep saying really. Is wow okay?" Her heart was expanding in her chest with his every word. What had she ever done in her life to be rewarded with a man like Craig Baron falling in love with her?

"You two had quite the day?" Lila Baron looked up from the lacy crochet project in her lap.

The Governor set his newspaper on the table beside him. Some days Craig was convinced his grandfather was the last person on the planet who still read his news on paper and not online. "I heard they think the owl trouble was just kids."

"That's what the officer told us at the vet. When we went back to the site, the other officers confirmed that they'd found nothing to suggest otherwise."

"Though we did get some additional good news for the studio project." Squeezing his hand, Kate grinned with more enthusiasm than he'd expected from someone who originally was not at all happy with his plans for the property. "Now that the owls are not nesting, they're no longer an impediment to the project."

He inched closer to her, knowing he'd never be able to get close enough, but simply didn't want to let her go.

"Makes sense," his grandmother said.

"Yes." Kate leaned her shoulder against him, silently communicating that she felt the same way about him. "And there's good news on the bat front. Whether it was merely timing or all the commotion, we can't be sure of, but the last of the hibernating bats is no longer hibernating. By the time construction is ready to begin, the bats should all have left the nest."

"Oh, that is good news." Grams leaned over to scratch behind the ears of the growing puppy at her side. "Despite the rocky start, this is turning out to be a glorious day."

"And that's not all." Still leaning against him, Kate let go of his hand and looped her arm around him. "My contact at Fish and Game says that the new guy has been reassigned without any repercussions for us after having moved the owl ourselves without permission."

Grams slapped her hands together and almost bounced out of her seat. "And the good news keeps coming!"

"Yes." The Governor nodded, then winked at Craig. There was no need for words. Both he and his grandfather knew darn well that his connections and name had most likely been at the crux of getting Mr. Rules-are-Rules reassigned and out of their hair.

And right now, Craig didn't even care if Ted came back. To his surprise, he didn't even care about the studio project. All he cared about was that Kate had said *I love you* back.

"Did you two have dinner?" his grandmother asked. "I can have Hazel warm something up for you."

"As a matter of fact, that's what we were hoping for." Craig pulled away from Kate and leaned over to kiss his grandmother on the cheek before straightening and once again taking firm hold of Kate's hand. "I'll let Hazel know we're going to eat on the veranda."

The evening was the perfect blend of crisp and warm for sitting outside. Besides, he liked the idea of being able to relax on a sofa that would accommodate both of them sitting close without a console between them.

Nestled on the outdoor sofa closest to the corner and away from the large windows, he draped his arm over her shoulder and kissed her cheek. "I wish we could stay here like this and didn't have to let go of you."

"Ditto. But it would make doing either of our jobs just a pinch difficult."

"Would it be awful of me to say I don't care?"

She shook her head. "Only because I feel the same way."

"Good. Because we're going to incorporate more habitat preservation policies into the studio design. Save the owls."

"And the bats." She grinned.

"And the bats." He kissed her temple. "And then I'm going to do my darndest to prove to you that I'm the perfect man for you."

Her fingers splayed across his chest, her chin tipped upward leveling her gaze with his. So much emotion danced in her eyes. "That won't be very hard. I already know all I need to know about you. I love you."

"Say that again." He kissed the tip of her nose.

"I already know all I need to know?" A teasing grin took over her face.

Shaking his head, he bit back a smile and drew her impossibly closer. "The other part."

"Oh, that. I love you."

"Thank heaven."

EPILOGUE

"This is the most perfect wedding ever."

The words that drifted across a huddle of guests brought a smile to Paige's face. Her sister Eve's wedding was the first large event held at the winery and even she was surprised at how few hitches they'd come across.

"Don't you look stunning tonight." Jack Preston, her sister's former party escort, came up beside her.

"Thank you. But no need to lay the flattery on so thick."

His eyes widened. "Sorry, was just stating a fact."

"Then I repeat. Thank you." Despite the stories of his youthful shenanigans with her brother Kyle and playboy reputation that followed him around all the rag magazines, she knew that Jack really was a stand-up guy. According to Eve, never once had he crossed the line with her and more than a few times, he'd saved her a world of headaches when it came to ambitious men eager to sink their teeth into the Baron assets.

"So what are your plans for the winery now?" he asked.

"Nothing new. We're just going to build on what we've got." Her cheeks tugged hard at her lips. "And it's going to be great."

Jack barked out a laugh that made his blue eyes sparkle. No wonder he was considered a catch. "It already is."

"And what are you two laughing about?" Mitch took a seat beside Jack. "And please don't tell me you're making a play for my kid sister. I'd hate to have to punch you in the nose."

Jack held up both hands. "Innocent."

"Mitch, leave him be. He's a perfect gentleman."

"See?" Jack smiled at Mitch.

While the two men started a new line of conversation over an upcoming bill that Mitch was sponsoring in the Senate, Paige's gaze scanned the room. The wedding planner was corralling her father away from the bar. Based on where Eve and Jared stood across the dance floor waiting, Paige knew their father's toast was next on the agenda.

Try as she might, she couldn't take her eyes off her sister and now brother-in-law. She'd seen their happiness all these months as their love took root and bloomed, and, of course, through the wedding planning, but somehow, she'd never seen them as much in love as they looked this very minute. They could barely keep their eyes, or hands, off each other. It was a joy to watch.

"Eve or Craig?" Her grandmother sat down beside her.

"Excuse me?"

"Which couple are you watching?"

"The bride and groom."

"Ah. I thought maybe it was Craig and Kate."

Pulling her attention away from her sister, she shifted her gaze left then right and spotted Craig and Kate at a nearby table. They were the only two still sitting while others danced. They sat so close that if Kate inched any closer she'd be sitting in Craig's lap. Their heads slightly down, she could tell they were sharing a private moment. One that had them both smiling. The whole scene made Paige grin. Though a small twinge of jealousy bloomed in her gut. So many of her siblings were finding their perfect match, and all of them looked so darn happy.

Keeping her gaze on her brother, she couldn't help but notice the gentle way his thumb caressed the hand he held while his eyes remained fixed on the woman he loved and the words she spoke. Where did a woman have to go to find a man to look at her like that?

"My money is on a June wedding." Her grandmother's gaze remained on her grandchildren.

"Did he propose?" Paige swung around to face her grandmother. How had she missed that? Surely someone would have told her.

"No." Her grandmother's grin widened. "But it's coming. I can tell."

Paige turned her attention back to what was now an empty table. Scanning the area quickly, she spotted her brother and his new love on the dance floor. They fit together perfectly. Again that tinge of jealousy pricked at her, but she would not let it soil how happy she was for all her siblings and their soul mates. Not only did Craig and Kate's silhouettes fit together like two pieces to a puzzle, Paige had never seen Craig look so good on a dance floor. The two bodies swayed as one, and then when she least expected it, Craig would twirl Kate out and back into the fold of his arms. Every time Kate's smile grew, and Paige would swear she could see the bright twinkle in the woman's eyes all the way across the room.

She had to agree with Grams. No way those two were going to make it much longer without self combusting. Yep, her money was also on a June wedding.

"Look." Her grandmother pointed across the hall. "Eve's lining up to toss the bouquet."

Glancing in the direction her grandmother's finger pointed, Paige spotted the line-up. Apparently, the coordinator gave up on her father.

"Go on." Grams nudged her arm.

"That's silly."

"Maybe. But it's your sister's wedding. Go."

"Yes, ma'am." Paige saluted the family matriarch and took her place in a long line of giddy single women waiting for the longstanding, and in Paige's mind, silly tradition of the one to catch the bouquet would be the next to marry.

Standing as far away from the line as she could and still looking like she was eagerly participating, Paige listened to the countdown. *Three... two...* Someone beside her screeched so loudly in anticipation that Paige wondered if she'd be able to hear the rest of the night. The disc jockey called out *one* and Paige decided maybe the girl hadn't screamed all that loud after all. Barely lifting her hands, preparing to clap for the lucky—or unlucky—winner, her heart nearly leaped to her throat when the throwaway bouquet landed squarely between her hands.

Snapping her gaze upward, she spotted her sister grinning at her like the cat who'd eaten the canary. Great. This was all she needed. For the rest of the night everyone and their grandmother, especially *her* grandmother, was going to be ragging her about being next to wed. All the fuss and fawning on Craig and his new love would be forgotten as she'd be new fodder for the gossips. Oh well.

"See?" Her grandmother came up beside her. "Wasn't that fun?"

"Yes, Grams."

"Now you'll have to keep your eyes open. Maybe Mr. Right is here and you just haven't met him yet."

"Thanks, Grams." She refrained from shaking her head or gagging. She already knew every available bachelor on the Houston social registry and was less than enthusiastic about the prospects of finding a forever love anytime soon. For now, her only focus was growing the winery. Romance would have to wait. Glancing down at the round white bouquet in her hands, she got a sweet whiff of the floral scents, closed her eyes and fighting that twinge in her gut again, for just a second, let herself think, *if only*.

Enjoy an excerpt from
Just One Taste

"Find anything today you didn't see yesterday?"

When Paige Baron took over the family's interest in a large but failing Texas winery, the best part of the whole deal was Clay, the manager. Bless his heart, he'd done his best to hold the vineyard together for the former owners, but without the proper support, there hadn't been a chance in hell that he'd be able to keep up, never mind prosper.

"Maybe," she muttered, giving herself another moment to be sure.

"Do tell?" A man of few words, Clay was as old as the dirt beneath her feet, but worked harder than any two men half his age. Maybe three.

"I'm thinking it's time." She'd been staring at a barren strip of land adjacent to Baron property. Shortly after Baron Enterprises had purchased the old vineyard, Paige had been approached by a neighbor looking to make a killing on land no one else wanted. Being a woman, too many made the mistake of thinking she was a pushover. But more important than her gender, she was a Baron. Good business instincts were part of her gene pool. On the other hand, her ability to negotiate came from years of watching her older brothers wheel and deal the family's fortune from something already impressive into something bordering on obscene.

It had taken a good deal of playing cat and mouse with the arrogant neighbor, but in the end, they'd agreed on a price less outrageous and very reasonable. Every year as she implemented the next stage in her five year plan, she'd survey the land and think, not yet. This morning, when she stood on the veranda outside the new pavilion, her gut shouted at her for the first time. Dragging her gaze away from the untouched land, she looked to the guy who had been her right hand man since day one. "It's been three years."

Clay nodded at her. There was no need for her to explain, he knew she was talking about her prize hybrid grape. Or what she hoped would become an award winning new blend for the Baron Winery.

In her mind's eye she could see the bare acreage covered with rows of delicious plump grapes waiting to be turned into a fine wine. "We could do a limited edition." That was another thought that had been kicking around in the back of her mind as she considered the wine.

His gaze had drifted to the bare rolling hills. "We could."

Some days, she really hated that male tendency to barely utter a word. "Or?"

"No *or*." He shook his head and turned once again to face her. "It's a good plan."

That's what she wanted to hear. She trusted her gut more than anything, but a word of encouragement from Clay went a long way when it came to keeping her eye on the prize. "We've got multiple new bookings coming up for rather large weddings."

"Miss Eve's was a beautiful party." The older man hadn't known her sister for much longer than he'd known Paige, but he'd taken a shine to the whole family.

"I think there will be enough in the coffers to plant the new grapes."

"The French grape?"

She bobbed her head. Years of traveling the French countryside had brought her in contact with a good many vintners. Some more friendly than others. A few, fearing no competition from the young American female, shared their secrets. One in particular, an aging man who made her grandfather look like a spring chicken, and who swore Paige was the spitting image of his long deceased daughter, promised her when the time was right she could bring his cuttings stateside. If all went as she hoped, in a few more years she'd have sturdy vines and then, given a little more time, she could present the world with a new stellar Baron blend. The mere thought gave her goose bumps.

"You very busy?" The Governor's voice boomed strongly over her shoulder.

Paige swung around and took a few steps forward, enveloping her grandfather in a hug much the way she'd done since she was a little girl. "I've always got time for you."

The old man beamed. "Good. If I could have a few minutes of your time."

Clay cleared his throat. "I need to check on the new girl in the tasting room."

The former governor of the great state of Texas sidled up beside Paige. "Rumor has it the Comets are looking to move their franchise."

Her gaze narrowed as she quickly shifted her thoughts from wine to sports, taking a moment longer to place the name. "Hockey."

"Yes. NHL." The older man dipped his chin slightly. "We've been working on bringing a farm team to Houston, but if we could land the Comets…"

His words drifted off but Paige could see the twinkle in her grandfather's eyes. She'd heard many a story of his childhood, spending winter breaks with all his cousins at his grandfather's home in Colorado. Playing ice hockey on the lake had been one of his fondest memories. No doubt her grandfather could see a Zamboni clearing the ice of their under used stadium in anticipation of a Stanley Cup game as clearly as she could see currently fallow land lined with lush grapes. Her grandfather was a visionary in many ways. He fought hard for his state for many years, and continued to do so for his city, county and state wherever time and money allowed.

"Convincing the northern yankee owners that the Gulf Coast is the perfect spot for relocation won't be easy."

"Money talks." It was one of the first things she'd learned as a Baron. The second thing she'd learned was to use the Baron money for the greater good. Not always an easy task.

"I understand that Daniel Dupree is heading the initial vetting committee."

"The name sounds familiar." She couldn't quite put her finger on it.

"Canadian, played for the Bruins, then the Comets. MVP goalie three Stanley Cups in a row. His career was sidelined when a car accident crushed one leg. They saved the leg, but not his career."

Of course. "He and his brother used to play on the same team. Mitch was probably their biggest fan."

The Governor nodded. "It's my understanding that Dupree is personally visiting the competing cities."

"Is Houston one of them?"

"We're working on it."

Thoughts danced around in her head but none explained why her grandfather was sharing this with her of all people. She knew wine, not hockey.

Her grandfather rolled back on his heels and blew out a soft breath. "One thing I've learned in my life, politically correct or not—a woman in the room helps keep hot-headed men civil."

"Maybe."

"No maybe about it. Eve can't participate and Siobhan's off taking photos of African elephants. Can I count on your help?"

They could put all she knew about ice hockey in the proverbial thimble, but if her grandfather thought she could help… "Absolutely."

Ten cities and now Houston. It had taken Daniel the better part of the last few weeks to eliminate a slew of cities from the running and narrow it down to the best town, now eleven. Most had lofty ambitions without the financial backing his team wanted. As much as he disliked adding another city to his list instead of culling it, the last minute proposal from Houston had everything the team was looking for. Including an already built stadium, a little small, but suitable for ice hockey. No need to haggle with communities and bond proposals to bring the team in. Still, somehow his inclination remained geared toward a cold weather state without an annual hurricane season like Utah or Wyoming. Utah being the only one of the two on the shorter list. Unfortunately, Wyoming was out. Making the math work for a state that had more antelope than people simply didn't compute.

An existing unused stadium wasn't the only thing Houston had in its favor. Daniel had to admit the idea of an in state rivalry between two hockey teams mirroring the profitable rivalry between the two Pennsylvania teams piqued his interest. The revenue possibilities were enough to make a man drool. On the other hand, the lack of fans in recent games only bolstered the idea that the South was no place for multiple hockey franchises. Maybe.

"You ready?" Kevin, Daniel's right hand on this project, stood in the doorway.

Daniel glanced at his wrist watch. The flight to Utah left in a little under four hours. Just enough time to get to the airport and hurry up to stand in line and weed his way through security. "As ready as I'll ever be."

Kevin slid a piece of paper onto Daniel's desk. "This just came in. New Mexico is withdrawing the bid."

Looking at the sheet in front of him, Daniel bobbed his head. "Wonder who changed their mind?"

"No clue."

From the beginning Daniel wondered how the heck a state with only a few million people wound up on the list. All he could conclude is that someone in New Mexico had extraordinarily deep pockets. Now he wondered what made them change their mind and lock up their bank account?

"Do you have the data for the new addition?"

It took him a few moments to realize that Kevin was referring to Houston and not some other city the owners were thrusting upon him. "All I know is that Governor

Baron is one of the backers. Which probably explains why Houston is the only bidder coughing up the cost of a five star hotel."

"Surely Texas isn't the only one with deep pockets."

Daniel shrugged. "No, but they do say everything is bigger in Texas. It will be interesting to see what they have planned."

"I wonder if they're going to pick you up in one of those stretch limos with cow horns on the grill?"

"Unlikely. I'm renting a car. Besides, I'm pretty sure the horns are only from bulls."

"Nope. The longhorn cattle all have horns. No chauvinism among those bovines."

Daniel chuckled. "Noted." Though why his assistant from Brooklyn knew anything about Texas cattle was beyond him.

"Want some aspirin?"

Not till Kevin asked did Daniel realize he'd been rubbing his knee. When the drunken idiot who ran the red light smashed into the driver side of his car and sent it flying across the intersection into a lamppost, he thought his life was coming to an end. Thanks to a top notch trauma team and his brilliant surgeon, his life was saved, but not his career. After all these years, rubbing away the discomfort in his left leg was so common place, he didn't even realize that his leg had been bothering him. At least not till Kevin went into mother hen mode. For a guy, he was pretty good at noticing little things. "Nah, it's nothing."

His assistant didn't say another word about his leg, merely handed him a fat envelope with al the basic data for every city. Daniel had it all on his laptop, but on plane rides, he preferred to study the information on old fashioned paper instead of a backlit screen. His first assignment was to learn all about the former governor, the committee, the city, and anything that would help him get through this visit sooner than later. Someone may have convinced the committee to allot more days in Houston than any other city on the list, but as far as he was concerned, the quicker he could race through this visit the better. Shaking his head, he stuffed the envelope into his briefcase. How the heck did anyone expect to successfully mix ice hockey and a million degrees heat nine months of the year? Despite the lure of the in state rivalry, he was pretty sure he'd already made up his mind. The team needed a cold weather climate where hockey was in the city's blood. There was no way Houston had enough people to create a buzz around hockey. He seriously doubted that the sprawling city would hold any interesting surprises for him. Nope, Houston would definitely be a waste of his time.

Read more of Just One Taste available now

MEET CHRIS

Author of dozens of contemporary novels, including the award winning Aloha Series, Chris Keniston lives in suburban Dallas with her husband, two human children, and two canine children. Though she loves her puppies equally, she admits being especially attached to her German Shepherd rescue. After all, even dogs deserve a happily ever after.

More on Chris and her books can be found at www.chriskeniston.com.

Follow Chris on facebook at ChrisKenistonAuthor or on twitter @ckenistonauthor.

Join Chris' newsletter! Enjoy inside peeks and photographs from Chris' world and stories. Some times she'll thank her subscribers with a free copy of a new 99 cent flirt.

Please, if you enjoyed reading Just One Take, consider helping other readers find the Billionaire Barons of Texas Series by taking a moment to leave a review. Reviews are a blessing to authors and readers alike. Even just a few words will do! Thank you.

www.ingramcontent.com/pod-product-compliance
Lightning Source LLC
Chambersburg PA
CBHW020044310726
48970CB00007B/2409